Danger, lies, and betrayal forge the path to unlocking the secrets Brenn seeks.

The rescue of Brenn's pride sets off an angry tirade from Cewrick that results in curses that almost cripple the Crimson Realm and all of Ierilia.

With the help of Ciara, Brenn leads his crew through the bowels of the planet and the forbidden forest to unlock the secret of defeating Cewrick. But will his defeat end the reign of terror on their world?

The Dragon's Lion
Copyright © 2017 Taryn Jameson & Gabriella Bradley
ISBN: 978-1-4874-1693-5
Cover art by Angela Waters

Published by eXtasy Books Inc

Look for us online at:
www.eXtasybooks.com or www.devinedestinies.com

THE DRAGON'S LION
CRIMSON REALM CHRONICLES
BOOK 2

BY

TARYN JAMESON AND GABRIELLA BRADLEY

DEDICATION

Taryn Jameson

This one is for my co-writer and the crazy way our brains seem to work together. Without you, the Crimson Realms would not have been born. I look forward to continuing our journey through the realm.

Gabriella Bradley

For our readers. The rollercoaster ride through The Crimson Realm continues. We're having a lot of fun creating this world and all its characters. I hope our readers enjoy our crazy fantasies as much as we enjoy writing them!!

CHAPTER ONE

Brenn paced back and forth. How could he possibly rest after the events of the night? What had started out as a night of victory and discovery had quickly turned into one of disaster and havoc. Cewrick had vented his rage at losing his captives across the whole planet. Brenn's family and pride were safe, but at what cost? Even though Ciara had dispelled the wind funnels and their destruction, there was nothing she could do about the stone curse. So many innocents had turned to statues in a matter of minutes. If Cewrick unleashed the renegade Toubosians on the villages west of the Inar Ridge, they would have no defense against the ships and could suffer the same fate as Xynnar.

He stopped his pacing on the verandah of his rooms. Gazing over the courtyard, he caught a glimpse of his beautiful dragon as she slept in his orchard beneath the umbrella of his giant wraggia trees, their branches heavy and laden with ripe, lush fruit. He frowned, his brow creasing with worry for her. The night had taken its toll on Ciara. After flying to every corner of their planet to stop the black wind funnels, she had returned to Brenn's estate and tried every possible spell she could muster to halt the stone curse, but her magick had weakened. He could feel how weary she was, how helpless she felt against Cewrick. She rested now, too exhausted to fight the sleep that overtook her.

He hated that she fought alone. Dissipating the wind funnels had exposed her to more and more people. He knew word would travel to Cewrick about the jewel dragon protecting the Ierilians and he would realize it was Ciara, the sorceress that had escaped his clutches. He would know she was no longer bound to the Clyss, and the sorcerer would spare no effort in his attempts to find her so he could bespell her again and try to capture her for her much-coveted soul shard.

After the suns came up, the stone curse had stopped, but Brenn was sure Cewrick was brewing up more plans of revenge.

He was about to go and bathe when he spotted a swarm darkening the rays of the suns. Shading his eyes, he saw dozens of black dragons and urcals in the sky heading for the city. A bath was not important right now. An announcement needed to be made to the citizens of Cront to remain inside their homes. The dragons and birds could not pluck them from inside their dwellings. He quickly hailed Admiral Zhala on his communicator.

"Admiral, I apologize for contacting you this early, but a swarm of black dragons and urcals is approaching the city. A global warning needs to be issued as I'm sure this is happening in all our major cities on Ierilia."

"By the gods, I see them," the admiral uttered. "Leave it with me, Brenn. I just hope it is not too late for some. I'll send my fleet to annihilate them."

"No. You can't do that," Brenn warned him.

"I can't? What is—"

"Those black dragons, or many of them, were once jewel dragons, Ciara's parents among them. They have lost their humanity, but when the curse is lifted, they will return to their natural state. We cannot kill them. The urcals, yes. But they are flying together as one flock," Brenn explained.

"By the gods! What are we to do?"

"Stay inside. If they can't grab people to bring to Cewrick, they will surely give up."

"This is frustrating. We have the power to kill them all. But after what you told me, I won't attack. I have no wish to destroy jewel dragons."

"We also need to issue a warning for people not to touch the stone statues. They could break. Imagine when the curse is lifted, and people are missing arms or legs, or worse, if broken in half or missing their heads."

"Yes. We need to dispatch teams across the planet to transport the statues to safe holding areas. I fear it will prove quite an impossible task unless our people can all pitch in. There are far too many villages and outlying farms that suffered the curse." The admiral paused for a moment. "Let me get in touch with our media offices to get word out about the dragons and urcals and a message to the population to take great care in handling the statues. I'll be in contact."

Brenn feared for Ciara. As long as she remained sleeping, the black dragons and urcals could not see her from above. But what if she woke up and ventured into the courtyard?

After a quick wash and dressing, he opened his door to find Laro and Ivran about to knock, as well as Tomas standing behind them.

"Have you seen the black dragons, Brenn?" Laro asked.

Brenn was relieved to see Laro had returned from picking up Tomas. "It is good to see you are safe, my friend," Brenn said as he embraced Laro. "Yes, and the urcals. I have already been in contact with the admiral."

"What else is Cewrick going to hit us with in his wrath?" Ivran asked.

"I worry about Ciara. She is sleeping in my orchard, so she can't be seen from above, but what if she wakes? Cewrick knows by now that she is free from the Clyss."

"Can't she hide elsewhere? The Tideless Abyss, her natural habitat?" Laro asked.

"I don't know. Once the danger has dissipated, I will talk to her. Just help me pray to Taella, the goddess of tranquility, that Ciara sleeps for some time. I must warn my staff not to venture outside." Brenn quickly headed for the kitchens and hoped he wasn't too late as he could hear the flapping of wings above his house.

Just as he entered the kitchens, he heard a loud scream. Rushing to the window, he watched helplessly as several of his staff and some children were scooped up. He turned to face the staff already in the kitchen. "Under no condition are any of you to venture outside," he said sternly.

Gieth, his main cook, had tears soaking her chubby face. "They took my Nebly and my Elwin," she told Brenn in a trembling voice.

"I am so sorry, Gieth." No words could comfort the distraught woman who was joined by several other weeping women. Their children were taken, too.

"Why has that monster sorcerer unleashed his demon dragons and birds?" a kitchen helper shouted. "Something has happened to anger Cewrick."

"Yes, and the king is aware, as is Admiral Zhala. All of you know we are helpless against sorcery, but because of a recent, major transgression on his part, we have now declared war upon Cewrick and his minions. We will no longer fear his magick and shall defeat that monster once and for all time. Are there any of our staff members still to come, or are they all inside the main house now?"

"Yes. The household staff is. We begin our duties before the suns rise, but some of the gardeners need to be warned.

The children were about to go to school," Jastra, another kitchen helper, told him.

"Thank you, Jastra. Use the com system to warn the gardeners, please. I need you all to remain calm and inside until the dragons and urcals are tired of searching for victims. They can't stay up in the sky forever," Brenn told them.

"There is a lot you are not telling us," Oncith commented, a young lad Brenn had recently hired to work in his orchard. Most of the staff was present in the kitchens for their breakfast. Only a few of his gardeners were missing.

"You are correct, Oncith. But the less you know, the better. Just rest assured that the king, the admiral, and I are working on a plan." Brenn again tried to reassure them all. "My guests are already awake, so you can serve breakfast anytime," he told Gieth, but doubted she could function in her sorrow.

Brenn left them, his heart breaking for those whose children had been taken. Before going to the dining room, he looked out the windows but saw Ciara still fast asleep.

The staff had already set the table, and the dining hall was filled with the aroma of baked bread waiting for them on large platters. Dishes were filled with freshly churned butoro. It didn't take too long for two of the kitchen staff to enter carrying trays laden with various fruits and what smelled like smoked wolpertinger pie. The pie was filled with succulent pieces of wolpertinger, a bird with a large meaty breast. It was smoked slow in a fire pit, wrapped in wraggia leaves, the leaves of the fruit tree giving the meat a sweetened taste that paired well with the vegetables and the salty pastry of the pie. It was one of his favorites for breakfast, along with fried penghou eggs. The pretty pink delicacies were laid by the penghou birds, an exotic species that roamed free on his property. He was surprised because he thought the cook was far too emotional to function. Maybe some of the other kitchen staff had cooked. He didn't think he was hungry, but he managed to eat quite a bit of the appetizing meal.

His communicator buzzed. Answering it quickly, he greeted the king. "Biryn. I know why you are calling."

"I need you to come to the palace as soon as it is safe. Admiral Zhala will come as well. Come directly to my private quarters."

"I'll be there as soon as the dragons and urcals are gone."

"Can we be in on this?" Ivran asked.

"Let me meet with the king and the admiral first. Don't worry. I will keep you informed," Brenn told his friends.

He wondered how long it would take for the black dragons and urcals to tire of searching for victims.

It took several hours before the threat was gone. At least it seemed to be for the time being. Who knew what else Cewrick had up his robes. Before leaving for the palace, Brenn checked on Ciara one more time. She lay so still, he feared something was wrong, but then her tail curled around her body. She was merely in a deep sleep of exhaustion.

On his way to the palace, she suddenly contacted him. *Brenn, why didn't you wake me? I just woke up and know what has happened.*

"What could you have done, Ciara? You are one jewel dragon against a swarm of black dragons and urcals."

I could have stopped the urcals from abducting the children. I can best at least one of those monsters.

"And risk the rest of them going back to Cewrick with more information about you? Keep safe, my jewel dragon. Stay under the wraggia trees. We can't have a stray black dragon or urcal see you. Rest. You need it."

As he parked his hovercraft on the palace grounds, Ciara remained quiet. He hoped she would do as he had told her — rest. Hurrying up the steps, the guards opened the doors for him, and he went directly to the king's quarters.

CHAPTER TWO

The king quickly stepped toward Brenn and hugged him. "It is good to see you, my friend. The rescue went well."

"Yes, but now we face Cewrick's wrath, as you have witnessed," Brenn answered, disengaging from the hug.

Biryn filled three goblets with wine. "Aldis should be here any moment," he told Brenn.

He'd no sooner spoken, and the admiral arrived. "Aldis, congratulations on a successful mission," the king exclaimed, holding out a goblet.

"The praise goes to Brenn and his men. He told me to stay with the ship," the admiral grumbled.

"And for good reason, I presume?" The king looked at Brenn.

"The admiral is not used to ground missions or combat. I did not want to risk his life," Brenn told Biryn.

"Good decision. But now we face the wrath of the sorcerer. Cewrick has unleashed his minions upon us. Aldis, why didn't you annihilate the swarm of black dragons and urcals?"

"Brenn told me that many of the black dragons were once jewel dragons or humans. When the curse is lifted, they will return to their former state. Since the urcals and dragons flew as a flock, I could not attack," Aldis explained.

"I would not see the jewel dragons harmed or any humans.

I abide by the decision, but many of Ierilia's people were abducted before the warning transmission went out. What do you suggest we do in case of another attack?" the king asked.

"Cewrick's attacks can come in many forms. He has spies among us. He could use his magick and create other spells, or he could use his black dragons and urcals to attack again," Brenn said.

"What about your jewel dragon? Can she not help?" the king wondered.

"No, not against a swarm of them. She is but one and feeling helpless right now. It took a lot of her energy to fight the black wind funnels. She could not undo the stone curse. Her magick cannot come into full force until Cewrick is slain. And there is only one that can help us annihilate him," Brenn said.

"Who?"

"His son."

"Cewrick has a son? That is news to me," Biryn said.

"Your Majesty, I have not had the time to tell you everything. One of Aldis' spies who is a resident in Cewrick's castle was able to get him to divulge secrets. The goddess of magick, Rania, bore a child that was fathered by a human. It was a girl named Hirsuta, reported to be exquisitely beautiful. The child was raised on Ierilia by her human father. Cewrick met the young woman and was enamored by her beauty. He placed a spell on Hirsuta so she would agree to wed him. Soon after, Hirsuta was with child. Even though Hirsuta had gone against Rania and wed Cewrick, the goddess still favored her daughter and her grandchild. Rania blessed the boy to have more power and stronger sorcery than his father would ever have. Rania swore her daughter to secrecy to never tell Cewrick about the gift bestowed upon the infant.

"Hirsuta had become very close to Cewrick's brother. She broke her vow of secrecy and told him the child, upon coming of age, would be more powerful than Cewrick. She swore the brother to keep her secret. The brother broke his promise when the boy was in his teens. He told Cewrick. In his wrath, Cewrick killed Hirsuta and his brother, and then cursed the boy to the very bowels of Ierilia. The boy lives there as some kind of giant monster worm."

"I find it strange that the goddess allowed all this to happen to her child and grandson. He would be a boy no longer, I presume," the king said.

Aldis nodded. "It appears only the son is able to defeat Cewrick if he were to be released and the curse lifted. If the curse were lifted, he would be a man now. Why the goddess allowed it to happen, only the gods and goddesses know, but we are given a will of our own and sometimes have to live with decisions we make and the consequences. Perhaps the goddess didn't know of the love spell placed on Hirsuta."

"Truly spoken. And I presume only Cewrick is able to lift the curse?" the king asked.

"I can talk to Ciara, though her magick is weak until she herself is released from Cewrick's curse," Brenn said.

"So this would be a mission to release the son from his imprisonment," the king stated.

"Yes. Impossible. No one has ever traveled to the bowels of our planet. I did not even know such tunnels existed until now," Aldis said.

"There is always a first time," Brenn murmured.

Aldis snorted. "And so you find a gigantic worm, and you expect it not to eat you? That creature will not have any humanity left, no brain. If you can even go that deep down into the planet."

"We can but try. I am willing. I will do anything to save our people from Cewrick," Brenn said.

This curse was placed on the boy using very old magick. By the time Rania found out what had happened, she could not undo it because of the curses Cewrick placed everywhere. I heard Biryn's words. He is correct in saying that we are all given a will of our own. From what I know, Rania's daughter wed Cewrick against her mother's advice and had to suffer the consequences. Hirsuta foolishly talked about the gift Rania had bestowed upon her grandson. The gods and goddesses are not permitted to interfere in life's course. They can only help if we beseech them to assist us. The boy would have been raised to have no knowledge of Rania.

Brenn's ears perked up. "Are you able help us?"

The king and the admiral both looked at him, perplexed. "Brenn?" the king asked.

"Sorry. Ciara is speaking to me."

Yes. There is a potion to counter the curse. I can give you the ingredients you need to find. If you can get the worm to drink the potion, the worm curse will be lifted. But your journey deep into the planet will be fraught with danger. There are many creatures lurking in those tunnels. I cannot accompany you there. The tunnels do not accommodate my size. Neither can I help you. As I have told you many times, my magick is weak and cannot penetrate the many layers of the planet's crust.

"Ciara just told me there is a potion to counter the curse. She can give me the ingredients, but the worm has to drink the potion," Brenn told the men.

King Biryn's face lit up. "That sounds promising. But from what you tell me, it is a dangerous mission. And how you propose to feed a potion to a giant dangerous worm creature is beyond me."

"Yes, it is perilous. Ciara said the path would be fraught with much danger," Brenn said. "But I will do it."

"And I am with you," Aldis said.

"No. I cannot risk both my admiral and my general on such a hazardous mission. We can send others," the king responded.

"No. We don't know who to trust. Cewrick has loyal

followers planted everywhere among us. I will lead this mission. It is not often I do not follow your orders, Biryn, but in this case, I am disobeying you," Brenn said firmly.

"And I am accompanying you," Aldis said.

"And I suppose if I issue a royal order, you will still disobey it," the king said and sighed. "Brenn, get the ingredients and formula from your jewel dragon off to my scientists. Have them prepare the potion."

"Yes, Your Majesty," Brenn answered. "Ciara will remain here to try to protect everyone and help however she can."

"Brenn, stop it with formally addressing me. I am not at all sure about allowing you to go on this mission, but is there anything I can do to stop you? I know you too well. Nothing will deter you," Biryn stated. "But I am not in favor of you going along on this mission, Aldis. If you disobey me, I may strip you of your admiral rank."

"See if I care." Aldis smirked. "I am tired of sitting in an office and issuing orders. I want to be out in the field, whether it is in space or on the ground. And since this happens to be a ground mission, then so be it."

"More like an underground mission. You know I could clap you in irons for this," the king told him.

"And you will not do that. I know you too well," Aldis retorted.

"What in the gods' names would I do if both my general and my admiral succumbed to underground monsters? Can't I talk sense into either of you?" the king demanded.

Brenn managed a wry grin. "No, Biryn. My mind is made up."

"As is mine," Aldis echoed.

"I will return to my estate and get the list of ingredients and the formula from Ciara and will send it to the science building forthwith. As soon as they inform me that the potion is ready, I will assemble a team to begin our trek to the center of Ierilia," Brenn told them both.

"We have always known of the sorcerer and his magick, but he has been relatively quiet for centuries, just hiding in his castle," the king said. "I thought he might be getting very old and his magick waning. Meanwhile, he has been plotting and scheming. I truly abhor anything and everything to do with magick or sorcery. After this is all over, I will gather my court, and we will write new laws."

"Your Majesty, Ciara is good. She has helped us, healed me when I should have died. She healed a baby. She was able to use her magick to ward off the funnels. Like among humans, there is good and evil among other species, light and dark magick. Please, do not compare Ciara to Cewrick," Brenn begged.

"Nevertheless, all of it is sorcery. The son reportedly can overthrow Cewrick, but who is to say the son will not be worse than the father?"

"I understand your fear, Biryn," Brenn said. "Please do not make hasty decisions now. Let us see what the future brings."

Biryn stopped pacing and raised his goblet. "As always, your counsel is wise. Will there be a way to keep me informed once you enter the tunnels?"

"No, Your Majesty. All communication will be blocked," Aldis said.

The king wanted to know all the details of the rescue the previous day and kept them talking for a very long time. Brenn was glad when Biryn finally announced he was tired.

"Keep me informed as long as you can. May the gods be with you all."

CHAPTER THREE

Brenn could hardly wait to return to his home. He needed to communicate with Ciara and write down the ingredients and formula for the potion. His mind was plagued with some doubts. What if the ingredients were difficult to obtain? What if the king's scientists could not make the potion exactly as it should be? The suns were ready to set. He had not realized how much time he'd spent at the palace. Then again, after their official business, Biryn had demanded to know everything about their last mission, so the three of them had talked for hours.

Brenn could hardly wait to see Ciara, but he would have to wait until after sunset and everyone had gone to bed for the night.

He found his family and friends waiting, eager for news. The dinner table had been set, and the aroma of smoked meat entered his nostrils. Only now did he realize that all he had consumed that day was an early snack and the king's wine. His stomach rumbled.

I am happy you are home, my warrior. I listened to your conversation with the king. It is nightfall. Tomorrow, before the suns rise, I will give you the ingredients and the formula for the potion. Go and spend time with your family now, nourish your body. I will see you in your chambers later tonight.

Brenn's heart sped up at the thought of holding her in his

arms again. His meal couldn't end quick enough. But he knew his friends and family waited to hear of his meeting with the king.

"Until later, my dragon princess," he whispered.

Brenn looked around the room at his family and friends, noting that Tomas and Shanina had chosen to eat out on the verandah with Twink. He wasn't comfortable with it but thought it best that way. The adults had much to discuss. *I will keep the young ones safe, my love. They will come to no harm,* Ciara whispered to him. He knew she would do exactly that. Tomas and Shanina would be protected.

"What news do you have from King Biryn?" Laro asked.

"How do we plan on stopping Cewrick? How are we going to help the people that were turned to stone?" Ivran asked at the same time.

Brenn halted their questioning. "I know you are impatient to hear everything. I have much to tell you and will try to answer everything, but you must give me a chance to speak."

Brenn seated himself at the table with his friends and family. "Cewrick has a son. From what Aldis' spies have said, his son is the only one that can defeat Cewrick, but the son is cursed."

"A son!" Yartah exclaimed. "I have never heard this. And I have lived for many years."

"Where is this son? How do we know he does not assist his father?" Ivran asked.

"Cewrick placed a curse upon his son. At birth, the son was secretly blessed and gifted by the goddess Rania with powers stronger than Cewrick. When he found out, this angered the sorcerer so much, he turned the boy into a giant worm and cast him into the bowels of Ierilia. Our only hope of defeating Cewrick and stopping him is the rescue of his son."

"And how do you suggest we do that?" Laro asked.

"Ciara knows of a potion to break the worm curse. She will

14

give me the ingredients and formula tonight. After the potion is made, we will descend into the tunnels leading to the planet's center, get the worm to drink the potion, and bring Cewrick's son with us after he is transformed back to human," Brenn informed them.

"Just like that?" Laro asked, shaking his head. "Well, I am going with you. Someone has to save you from your madness."

"I am, too. I will not be left out!" Ivran stated.

"What about your families?" Brenn asked. "Ivran, you just had your family returned to you, and Laro, you are all Tomas has."

Ivran shook his head. "What about your family? And Ciara? *You* are my family, too. I couldn't live with myself if I stayed behind... safe... while you take all the risks."

"Our families will understand," Laro said.

"I agree with Laro and Ivran. You will accomplish much more working together on this mission than you would by leaving them behind," Yartah said. "Besides, even though they had a hand in our rescue, I do not trust the fleet fully. I cannot help but think there may be a traitor among them, or even more than one, followers of Cewrick."

"Listen to your father's wisdom in this, Brenn," Calene told him as she rested her hand on his arm. "I fear for your safety and that of Ivran and Laro. I will feel much better knowing you are on this mission together. You will keep each other safe from harm."

Reana spoke up next. "I, too, can put aside my fears. Cewrick unleashed his wrath because you saved us from him. If you hadn't come for us, these attacks would not have happened. Knowing that it is your plan to destroy Cewrick, Ivran and I have already discussed him accompanying you on another mission."

"Fine, you both can accompany me on the mission," Brenn

said as he looked at Ivran then Laro. "I do not like it, but I will speak to Aldis and ensure you are both present when we plan our strategy."

"Let us eat and enjoy this short reprieve we have been blessed with," Yartah said. "I do not think it will last for long."

Brenn hoped that the reprieve would last for more than a few hours. He had much to discuss with Ciara, and he longed to hold her in his arms, to know she was safe, at least for a little while. He finished his meal, pushed away from the table, and walked to his parents to hug them both. "I am thankful you are both safe." Brenn could see the weariness in his parents' eyes. Their captivity had taken its toll on them as well as the current state of affairs.

Ivran and Laro had retired earlier to put the children to bed. Shanina, who had slept restlessly the night before, had gone off to her room, too. Brenn hoped that having her beloved pet home and safe would help dispel her nightmares.

"We should get some rest while we can," Brenn told his father and mother. "I have much to plan in the morning."

Brenn followed his parents out of the dining hall and made his way to his rooms, then walked out to the verandah that overlooked the orchards and rested his hand on the balustrade. "I need you, my dragon princess. I need to hold you in my arms and know that you are safe," he whispered as he looked out over the grounds.

A familiar fragrance entered his nostrils. He swung around and headed straight for his bed, instinctively knowing she would be waiting for him. He stopped for a moment to drink in the sight that met his gaze. His siren had somehow decorated the room with vases of red laceflowers. Their blooms were huge, their fragrance potent. She lay naked on his bed, petals strewn all over her body and the bedding, and her hair was spread out like a black velvet cloak.

Ciara smiled, showing her pearly teeth. "Come, my

warrior. Join me. It will be our last night together until your mission is completed."

Brenn didn't need a second invitation. His cock was already hard by just thinking about her. Seeing her like that had it throbbing in anticipation. He climbed onto the bed and knelt between her spread legs, her pussy open and waiting for him. The soft black fur that covered her swollen lips glistened with her cream. Brenn lowered his head and licked from her anus to her clit.

He had tasted women before, but none had ever tasted as sweet as his siren. For a moment, he sucked her hard nub before trailing kisses up her belly, to her breasts, to finally seek her parted lips. Wrapping his arms around her frail body, he kissed her, his tongue exploring every crevice of her mouth. He groaned when she sucked his tongue.

Suddenly, she pushed him away and onto his back. "My turn," she said softly. Kneeling between his legs, she fondled his cock, his taut sack, pushing and massaging the erogenous zone between his sack and his cock.

"If you don't stop, I will come," Brenn murmured, breathing hard, his heart hammering sending his blood coursing throughout his body. He groaned when her lips trailed up his cock, her tongue tracing the pulsing veins along his shaft, then circling the head. She took him into her mouth then, her tongue entering the hole, and she licked the pre-come that ran steadily from it. When she sucked him into her mouth and pushed down, he feared the length and girth of his cock would choke her, but she took him wholly. Her hands continued to fondle his sack, the base of his cock, while she sucked and moved the skin back and forth.

He didn't want to come inside her mouth, but trying to contain his release was almost impossible. "Turn around so I can pleasure you," he grunted in between heavy breaths to stop himself from coming.

Without releasing his cock, she swiveled her body and straddled him, the lips even more swollen and fully spread to expose her moist, succulent slit to his gaze and beckoning entrance. Placing his fingers on either side of the lips, he parted the labia and watched her pearly cream trickle slowly. It fascinated him. Unlike any woman he had been with in the past, her cream was translucent and had a mauve sheen to it. Neither was its scent musky but rather more like the perfume of a flower. He licked it, allowed it to rest on his tongue for a few moments. It was almost as if her juices acted as an aphrodisiac, because his ardor could hardly increase any more than at that moment. He entered a finger, then two, and explored the soft inner walls of her vagina. But this wasn't what he longed for. He needed to be one with her, to take her, for his cock to find its home.

Grabbing her by the waist, he pushed her off his body and onto the bed. In a second, he climbed between her legs. Then, as he entered her and her legs wrapped around him, he pushed inside her waiting warmth completely. He felt her squirm beneath him, push up to accommodate him. One thrust and he could hold back no longer. He shuddered, groaned loudly as he released, gratified that she moaned her release to match his.

Sated for now, they lay quietly for a little while, just holding each other, until he moved off her body and lay beside her. Leaning on his elbow, he gazed down at her beauty, at her tousled hair, her face rosy from the aftermath of her passion. He traced her eyebrows, her nose, her lips, and said softly, "I love you so much, my dragon princess. You have taken over my heart and soul."

"And I love you, my warrior," she whispered against his finger that rested on her lips, then kissed his fingertip.

She sat then and looked at him. "But we need to talk about the potion. Brenn, get your notebook so you can record what

I am about to say."

"Nothing like talk of potions and recording to douse a man's ardor." Reluctantly, he got off the bed and went to a desk in the corner of the room. He took the notebook out of a drawer, turned it on, and joined her. "It is ready to record, my love."

"These are the ingredients. Five drops of sea serpent venom, a thimble of sea water, ten drops of a dragon's tears, a dragon's scale, a pinch of yellow bark, two sprinkles of thunder leaves, a pinch of blister leaves. And now, the most important ingredient of all, blood from the clymm horse. The clymm horse is rare and only found in Clymm Valley, between the Clymm Mountains. One vial of blood from each side of the horse's cheeks. Grind all the solid ingredients into a fine powder, mix in the venom, the sea water, and dragon's tears, then heat slowly for half an hour. Mix the two vials of the blood. Then add the heated mixture to it. All ingredients must be exact, or the potion will not work. After it is completed, I will bespell it."

Ciara stopped and nodded for Brenn to stop recording. "Now you will need to find all the ingredients, Brenn."

"Such a simple task," he grumbled.

"You can designate some tasks to your friends," Ciara suggested.

"If we are to gather all the ingredients in good time, yes, we will all have to work together to find them all."

"I can fly you to Clymm Valley. But I must warn you, the clymm horse is not easy to catch," Ciara told him.

"And how do I extract blood from its cheeks?" Brenn asked. He had heard of the breed but had only seen a picture of them—a very big horse with six legs, like his pack horse. They were pure white in color. Their heads were a slightly different shape, and they had a fat cheek on either side of their face, almost like pouches.

19

Ciara laughed. "Not easily. The blood pouches are for their young. They only give birth to one foal every ten years. For the foal to survive, it needs the nourishment from this special blood that is stored in the cheeks during gestation. Each cheek has a small nipple. It is like milking a jago for milk, except the nipples are much smaller."

"Oh, so that is even simpler. All I have to do is find a pregnant clymm horse or one that has just foaled. And it would just let me do that? And how do we obtain venom from a sea serpent?"

"The horses are quite tame. As for the serpents, they are in abundance in the Glahm Ocean, not too far from here."

"I guess a dragon's tears I will really have to search for, and a scale," Brynn jokingly said.

"You must rest now. We will leave at sunup for Clymm Valley. You must eat before that and give instructions to your friends to get the other ingredients," she told him, stroking his face while curling against him.

CHAPTER FOUR

Brenn awoke to find his arms empty. The suns had not yet risen, so where was Ciara?

You slept soundly, my love, and I did not want to entice you upon waking. I am beneath the wraggia trees in your orchard. There is no threat in the sky, but it is best to be cautious. After you have bathed, eaten, and given your friends their instructions, we will leave.

Brenn quickly bathed and dressed, wearing his warrior gear. Breakfast was not yet served, so he went to the kitchens to find some food. Only a few of the kitchen staff were there. He presumed Gieth would not be able to do her duties until her children were saved. One of Gieth's helpers warmed some leftover pie and cut him a chunk of fresh bread. He consumed it as fast as he could and drank a full mug of jago milk.

As he was getting ready to leave the kitchen, Laro, Ivran, Tomas, and Shanina entered the dining hall. The adolescents looked restless. They were used to being outdoors. At home, part of their daily activities included collecting herbs, berries, and fruits as well as hunting small game to supplement what was grown in the orchards and gardens.

"You look in a hurry. You weren't planning on leaving us behind, were you?" Laro asked.

"Actually, I was going to wake you. I have the formula and the list of ingredients we need. We will have to split up to collect them," Brenn said, then looked at the adolescents seated at the table. They were responsible enough to search the grounds for a couple of the easier items. "Shanina... Tomas... would you like to assist us on a quest?" he asked.

"Does that mean we get to go with you?" Tomas asked.

"Yes! Is the dragon coming?" Shanina asked at the same time.

"No, you are not coming with us, and Ciara will be with me. What I need you to do is to collect some yellow bark and thunder leaves out on the grounds. It is very important. We need them to make a potion. Can you do this for us?" Brenn asked.

"We can do it. It will be fun to explore outside, and Twink will enjoy being able to run and play," Shanina said.

Tomas nodded in agreement, his mouth full of wraggia fruit pastry the kitchen staff had set before him. The fruit was a favorite among his people. The large fruit had a thick, spiny shell that had to be broken to get to the juicy, purplish flesh inside. It had a fresh, light taste that melted in your mouth.

"Good. I knew I could count on you," Brenn said as he smiled at them. He turned to Laro and Ivran. "Walk with me. I have a long journey ahead and must meet Ciara in the courtyard shortly."

Laro and Ivran followed Brenn to the courtyard outside. The suns were peeking over the horizon, the sky filled with hues of pink, orange, and mauves. The beauty of it would take anyone's breath away, and after the past day, Brenn was thankful for the peaceful morning. "Ciara and I will collect the clymm horse blood. I would like you to collect the sea serpent venom, sea water, and blister leaves."

"That is no easy task. I am sure the sea serpents would be more than willing to fill *us* with their venom instead of a vial," Ivran said.

"We will use you as bait," Laro joked to break some of the

tension. "Where will we find these sea serpents?"

"Ciara told me the Glahm Ocean is filled with them. I will notify Aldis. He will assist in collecting the venom."

Brenn picked up his communicator and called Aldis. "Admiral, I have the list of ingredients from Ciara. Laro and Ivran will meet you at your hovercraft in my courtyard. Be prepared. One of those items is venom from the deadly sea serpent. We will meet back at my estate after all the items have been collected."

"Just call me Aldis from now on. Thanks for the warning. I will make sure we have the needed equipment to capture one serpent and collect what we need. I will see you forthwith. Tell Ivran and Laro to be ready and waiting in the courtyard. And I will also have the vials for the blood for you."

"Thank you, Aldis," Brenn said as he closed the communicator and looked at Ivran and Laro. "There should be some blister plants growing in the grasses as you near the ocean. Collect several of the leaves. Be careful. They are not called blister plants for nothing. I am not sure how much a pinch would be for the potion. Better to have more than we need. That goes for the venom and sea water as well."

"I agree, I would hate to spill some of the venom and ruin our chances of making the potion correctly," Laro said.

Ivran looked at Laro. "I am ready to take on the great beast. Let's get this done as quickly as possible."

"Be careful, my friends. I hope we will have collected what we need and be back here by sunset at the latest," he told them as Laro and Ivran headed toward the landing spot for the hovercraft.

Brenn looked out over the courtyard and spotted Ciara waiting for him near the wraggia trees. His heart raced as he remembered the feel of her in his arms the night before. "I am ready, my love," he whispered.

As he made his way through the courtyard to meet her, his

communicator went off. Cursing, he stopped and opened it.

"Brenn," King Biryn's voice came over the communicator. "I have a request for you. Erica, the Earth captain, is being escorted to your estate as we speak. She wishes to assist us. You will allow her to."

"Biryn, I have no wish to put her life in peril. She is new to our planet. She has no idea what dangers we are facing."

"After the dragons and urcals, she has a good idea. We have had to explain much to her. Two of her people were taken. Her second-in-command, Mark, was among them. She understands the risks and has been picking up on our language pretty well, though she will still have to use a translator. I have updated her on the mission for the potion and told her about Cewrick's son."

I can bear both of you, my warrior. It will be safer for her to travel with us to collect the clymm blood than it would be for her to assist Ivran and Laro.

"I will abide by your wishes and will wait for her arrival. We have the list of ingredients we need for the potion. She can assist me in collecting the clymm horse blood," Brenn told Biryn.

"Good. She will be there shortly. And Brenn... be careful. I am still angry with you and Aldis, but I understand your need to head the mission and Aldis' need for action rather than be confined to an office all the time. Contact me when you return."

Brenn closed his communicator. He could hear a hovercraft approaching and assumed it was Erica's transport. He waited for it to land and hurried toward it to meet her. He had no wish for further delays.

He watched as the hovercraft landed. Erica stepped out of the open doorway and down the steps. She was no longer wearing her Earth clothing but instead wore an Ierilian space battle suit. She had cut her hair to a short style that formed wisps around her face, softening her features. The look suited her well, though it was unusual. He was used to Ierilian women all having long hair.

"Erica. Good morning," Brenn said. "Aldis should be here shortly to give me vials and pick up Ivran and Laro," he said as the craft took off.

Within seconds, another craft landed. It was Aldis. Brenn looked behind him to see Ivran and Laro hurrying toward the landed hovercraft.

Aldis stepped onto the first tread of the steps and held out a container. "Brenn, here are the vials."

Brenn hurried up the steps to get them. "Good luck, Aldis. Be careful."

"What is the Earth captain doing here?"

"She wants to help. The king ordered me to take her along, so she'll go with Ciara and me," Brenn told him.

After Ivran and Laro had entered the craft and it took off, he turned to Erica.

"Brenn, it's good to see you. Thank you for allowing me to assist," Erica said.

Brenn could see that the king had provided her with one of the fleet translators. Communicating with her would be much easier than using the translators from Earth. She did not have to hold it to her mouth or push a button, nor was he required to use one of his own.

"Come, we must hurry. Ciara awaits us in the orchard. She will fly us to Clymm Valley to collect the blood we need for the potion."

Erica gasped in surprise. "What do you mean fly us? Isn't Ciara the dragon?"

"Yes, she is," Brenn told her as he led her toward the orchard where Ciara waited.

His beautiful lifemate stood just outside the orchard, the suns' light shining on her scales causing a silvery-purple glow to surround her. He watched as she stretched both wings out and slowly moved them up and down, preparing for the long flight ahead.

"She's incredible!" Erica exclaimed. "She looks nothing like those awful creatures from yesterday."

I am ready, my love. You will have to help Erica onto my back. Ciara lowered her head to rub it against Brenn's neck, then kneeled to make it easier for them to climb up.

"She is indeed beautiful. Step into my hands. I will hoist you up. You will have to hold on to me while she is flying. I have no wish for you to fall from her back."

I can shield you both from falling. It is a gift all dragons have. You do not have to worry, my love.

Brenn helped Erica, then climbed up to seat himself in front of her. "We are ready," he said. Then to Ciara, *thank you, my dragon princess.* Brenn could feel a touch of magic as a shield settled itself around them, then a surge of power as Ciara lunged herself into the air.

Erica squealed behind him. "This is amazing! I can't believe I am riding a dragon! On Earth, they are only mentioned and pictured in fairy tales you read in books or see in movies."

Brenn laughed at her obvious delight. The captain appeared hard and unwavering in front of her crew, but she had an almost childlike innocence about her. He wondered about her crew members that had been taken but did not want to curb her joy by asking about them. He would wait until their mission was over.

"Ciara is the first I've seen of her kind. All I knew of were Cewrick's black dragons, and until now, we only saw those far in the distance above the sorcerer's castle and the forbidden forest."

"All this is still so hard to believe. It's like I'm in a fairy-tale dream," Erica said.

"I'm afraid it's all too real. Our king and our planet are in grave danger. If the sorcerer is able to gain power, Ierilia will no longer be the paradise planet it is now. It would become unbearable for those of us that do not follow him." Brenn spoke grimly. "Look what he did to the jewel dragons. From what Ciara has told me, they were living in complete peace in the Tideless Abyss, until Cewrick coveted the beautiful gems they mined and sold to the people of Ieralia to make jewelry. He could not destroy the Tideless Abyss, nor could he ever enter them to get what he wanted. So, in his wrath, he turned all jewel dragons into black dragons and took their soul shards. He was able to place a curse on them from afar. Ciara was the only one able to escape the black dragon curse by fleeing to Clyss Valley, but Cewrick placed a spell on her to contain her there."

"But now she is here. How did she escape that valley?"

"That is another whole story. We're almost there. Ciara is beginning to descend into Clymm Valley," he told her.

CHAPTER FIVE

Erica was a little unsteady as she slid down Ciara's neck. "I feel lightheaded," she told Brenn.

"The air is much thinner up high. You will be okay shortly," he said.

"Where are the horses? All I see are hills of grassland and more grassland. There are very few trees here," she commented.

They are grazing just on the other side of the hill. When we landed, I saw them. There are two horses expecting a foal, and I saw one very new foal among the group.

"Ciara just told me they're on the other side of this hill," Brenn told Erica.

"Are you sure they're tame?"

"Ciara assured me they are very friendly."

They climbed the hill through the tall grass, some of it reaching almost to Brenn's shoulders. When they got to the top, they saw the herd.

"Is this all of them?" Erica asked. "There only look to be about thirty or less."

"There are probably more behind other hills. From what I have learned, the families stay together. Because they can only foal once every ten years, their numbers don't increase fast."

"They're beautiful. If they had a horn and four legs, they

would resemble a unicorn. Are they all white?"

"Yes, they are all white. What is a unicorn?"

"A unicorn is another fairy-tale creature we read about on Earth."

After they got to the bottom of the hill, they carefully approached the herd. Some of the horses were grazing, others lying down. Brenn took the two large vials out of his bag and handed one to Erica. "I don't know how good you are at milking?"

"Milking?"

"Do you see those fat cheeks on the two horses ready to foal? They are filled with the blood we need. There is a small nipple on them. We need to extract the blood as if we were milking jago milk."

"You're kidding me."

"What does that mean?"

"You are joking."

Brenn laughed. "It's no joke. A newly born foal needs the blood to survive."

"That's the strangest thing I've ever heard," Erica grumbled. "And the horses will allow us?"

"I don't know. We are about to find out," Brenn said and carefully approached one of the expecting horses. He talked softly to it and hesitantly touched its face, then stroked its nose. The horse whinnied and rubbed her face against Brenn's hand as if she knew what he needed. "Very tame. You go ahead and approach the other horse."

He took the stopper off the vial, stuck it in his pocket, then gently prodded the large bulge. It felt almost like a woman's breast, except it had silky white fur all over it. He decided to treat it like Ciara's breast and kneaded carefully. The horse didn't seem to mind. As Brenn kneaded, red drops began to appear from a nipple in its center. He quickly held the vial close to the nipple until the red liquid ran out in a thin, steady stream. He continued to talk softly to the horse. His vial was almost full, so he glanced over at Erica. He noticed she was copying him and successfully collecting the blood.

"Our mission is easy. I wonder how the others are faring collecting the venom and blister plants," he commented to Erica.

When Laro and Ivran entered the hovercraft, Aldis told them, "I have to return to the science building to collect some equipment we need. It will be ready for us." He quickly punched in the coordinates, and they took off.

After entering the hovercraft chamber, the panel opened. Several officers were waiting to load the equipment. One piece looked to be a large harness attached to a heavy chain and the other a tranquilizer gun. The harness and chain took two men to carry.

"Let us help you load. We must leave quickly to make it back before sunset," Laro said as he and Ivran helped the men load the equipment into the hovercraft.

"That should be all of it. Let's get this mission over with," Aldis said as he seated himself at the controls and set a course for the Glahm Ocean. Laro and Ivran quickly took their seats.

"It shouldn't take us long to reach the Glahm," Aldis informed them.

"How are we supposed to get the venom from the sea serpent?" Ivran asked.

"That is what the harness and tranquilizer gun are for. We will have to lower one of you down after we have secured one of the serpents. You will then use these large vials to milk the venom from its fangs. When you hold the serpent's lip up you will see the fangs. Hold the vial so the tip of a fang is inside it.

Then use your thumb and massage the venom gland. The venom will release into the vial," Aldis said as he held up two empty vials.

Laro smiled at Ivran. "Oh, that sounds super easy. Told you we were going to use you as bait."

Aldis laughed at them. "We just might have to. We will have to lure one close enough to the shallow water to be able to tranquilize it and secure it long enough to milk some of the venom from its fangs. I will have to hold the hovercraft steady while one of you is lowered down to it. The other will have to be ready to shoot it again if it wakes."

"Ivran is a better shot, so I guess I am the bait," Laro said.

Aldis slowed the hovercraft over the ocean. "Keep your eye out over the water. As soon as we spot a serpent, I will lower the bait and lead it toward the shallows."

"There, over on the left. The water is swirling," Laro said, pointing down at some foamy water.

A long body broke through the surface of the water and slithered around before dropping back below, then swirled again.

"I'm dropping the bait now. That should get its attention," Aldis said as he maneuvered near where the sea serpent had surfaced.

"How do you know it will follow the bait?" Ivran asked.

"The bait consists of sea serpent pheromones. Works every time."

"Something tells me that you have done this before," Laro said as he and Ivran pulled the harness and tranquilizer gun out of the storage bay.

"My father used to hunt them. I went with him on many trips to acquire venom. It is not unheard of for fishermen to be bitten by them during hatching season, so our scientists need the venom to make the antidote. The females lay their eggs in the shallows, and when they hatch, the babies swim and feed there until they are large enough for the deeper waters."

"Why do we not catch one of the little ones? Wouldn't that be easier?" Laro asked.

"It is not hatching season, and I do not want to tangle with a female protecting her nest."

"Good point."

"Look! It's following the bait!" Ivran exclaimed.

Laro and Ivran watched as the huge sea serpent lunged toward the bait, following behind the hovercraft. Its blue scales glistened in the suns as it propelled its long body forward. It had a row of spikes lining the tip of its nose all the way down its back. The head was large, with several rows of serrated teeth and two huge fangs that retracted back into its mouth when it wasn't on the attack. Sea serpents wrapped their prey with their long bodies and sank their fangs into the victim's flesh to inject the venom. After the prey stopped moving, they ripped into it with their rows of sharp teeth.

"We are just about there. Ivran, help Laro into the harness. We will have to lower him through the door after you tranquilize the serpent. We will be hovering near it while you take your shot."

Ivran helped Laro into the harness, then secured the chain to the automated hydraulic system in the doorway. He picked up the tranquilizer gun and loaded it with several cartridges. "Is one shot enough to put it to sleep?"

"Yes, they are formulated to the sea serpent's biology. It should only take a few seconds to put it to sleep. Try to hit it in the back of the neck. You should be able to see its head now that we are in shallow water," Aldis told him as he opened the hovercraft's outer door.

Ivran braced himself at the open door. The water was shallow enough that the serpent's head and part of its long body protruded out of the water. He sighted the barrel of the gun on the serpent's neck, then pulled the trigger. Within seconds the body stopped writhing. The beast was asleep. "It's done."

Ivran hooked Laro's harness to the chain. Laro stepped out of the door and hung suspended for a moment before Aldis pushed the button to set the hydraulic gears into motion to begin lowering the basket. Slowly, Laro descended to the sleeping serpent. It was easy enough for him to stand in the water and walk over to its head while glancing around for more possible serpents. He took the large vial out of his pocket, uncapped it, and carefully lifted the side of the serpent's mouth to expose its fang. He put the tip of the fang into the vial and ran his thumb against the poison gland, stimulating the venom to flow and filling the vial. Placing the cap on the first vial, he took the second out of his pocket and did the same.

As he was removing the second vial from the tip of the fang, he felt the lip twitch against his hand. Its tongue slid against his fingers. He almost dropped the vial of venom as he jerked his hand away from the fang. He carefully capped the vial and placed it back into his pocket. Looking up at the hovercraft, he hurried toward it, not wanting to attract the beast's attention if it was waking.

"It's right behind you! Run!" Ivran yelled.

Laro started running as fast as the current would allow him, his heart beating so hard he thought it would burst through his rib cage. He had just climbed into the basket when he heard a shot firing from the tranquilizer gun. Then the chain went taut as he was pulled quickly to the doorway.

"Do you have it?" Ivran asked.

Laro held up the vials and smiled.

"That was close," Ivran said while shaking his head.

"You are going after the blister leaves. This was enough excitement for me," Laro told him.

Aldis laughed as he returned to the console. "There are some blister plants close to the coastline. We'll land there shortly."

The hovercraft landed close to a large patch of the plants. "Your turn. Be careful not to touch them," Laro said, handing Ivran a container.

Ivran grimaced and put on the protective gloves, then descended the steps and approached the patch. Just as he was about to bend to pick some of the leaves, a zacania spider jumped up at him. He stepped back, tripped over a rock, and fell, his arm landing among the blister plants. Ignoring the instant pain, he scrambled up and quickly ripped some of the leaves off the plants and placed them in the metal container.

"We need to get you back fast. That looks bad," Laro said as Ivran entered the craft.

"It feels bad. I hope Brenn and Erica don't meet with any danger."

"The clymm horses are tame. I am sure they're fine," Aldis told them as he set course for Brenn's estate.

"Thank you for this gift. It will hopefully help to save our world," Brenn whispered against the horse's head. He continued to talk to the horse for a little while, stroking her, patting her neck. When he stroked her huge belly, he felt the foal inside her kicking. It was a wondrous feeling. Several of the other horses had walked over to investigate the strangers among their midst. One of them nuzzled his neck.

"I think we've made friends," Erica said.

He looked at her and saw a group of horses surrounding her, too. "Yes, it appears we have. These horses never see humans. People have no interest in them because they do not reproduce fast enough so are not good for farm animals or to ride. Neither are there any other animals or humans in this valley, so the horses live here in peace."

It is time to leave, Brenn.

"Ciara said it's time to go. We need to say goodbye," Brenn told Erica. "Give me your vial, and I'll store it in my bag." He quickly placed both vials in his bag in the special cooling container Aldis had given him.

They said goodbye to the horses, Brenn almost reluctantly. "I would love to have one or two of them in my stables," he said.

"I don't have stables... yet, but I agree with you. But it would be sacrilegious to capture them and remove them from this valley," Erica agreed and sighed.

"I concur. Here, let me help you up." Brenn helped her climb onto Ciara, then climbed up himself. He loved the feel of her soft scales under his hands. Flapping her wings, Ciara leaped up into the sky and soared high.

"Oh, I wish she could fly me over the whole planet," Erica said behind him, hanging tightly on to his waist.

"You can't fall off, Erica. Ciara has a holding spell on us. It is safe to let go."

Tell your Earth friend when all is safe on our planet, I will be happy to give her a tour.

"Ciara just told me to tell you that once all danger is behind us, she will be happy to fly you across the planet."

"It's amazing how she speaks in your mind. But it seems only you can hear her. On Earth, there are books about shapeshifters that can communicate that way. I would almost think... what the hell is that?"

"It is a stray urcal. I know the holding spell surrounds us, but hold on to Ciara's scales tight," Brenn warned.

The urcal, as large as Ciara, if not bigger, came at them at full speed. Ciara slowed. Spikes appeared on top of her head and down her neck. Her color changed from beautiful jewel mauve and purple to a very dark purple all over. The urcal's large beak came toward the dragon to pierce Ciara's heart, its huge claws spread, ready to pluck the humans off Ciara as she would begin to tumble down.

Brenn's heart almost stopped as the beak was so close he thought his dragon princess had met her last moments. *Do not fear,* she whispered in his mind.

He felt her body tremble as she sucked in a huge breath. Within seconds, a stream of fire issued from her mouth, setting the urcal ablaze. It wavered. She blew fire at it again, until very little of the bird could be seen. It began to fall, a fiery ball, its screams echoing back to them.

Brenn did not realize he'd been holding his breath. He let it out in relief.

"My god. I thought we were done for," Erica shouted, her fingers digging into his waist.

"As long as there is only one stray beast and no more," Brenn muttered.

The flight continued. Now, Brenn kept gazing around to look for any specks above them or below. "I see something up above. Ciara, look up."

A stray black dragon came swooping down. Ciara dodged it, obviously not wanting to slay the dragon. Strangely enough, the dragon was about to attack Ciara when suddenly it stopped. It flew up, came back down, and stopped again. Ciara slowed down.

Brenn tried to figure out what was going on. "Ciara, I know you do not want to kill it, but if it grabs us—"

It is strange. It's as if this black dragon knows me. It could have attacked, tried to grab you both, but it is just hovering. I thought all humanity was gone from their minds, but it appears that this one has a semblance of it left.

"If so, ask it to go away. We need to get the ingredients

home safely," Brenn said.

It just communicated with me.

"What did it say?"

Ciara, help us. Please help us.

"Do you know who it is?"

No. It just keeps begging for help. I have tried to tell it that our mission is to do exactly that. I think it wants to help, too, but it fears Cewrick's wrath. He can incinerate the dragons in a second if they do not do his bidding. This dragon recognized me.

Brenn watched the black dragon hover a moment longer, then it soared up and flew away.

"That was interesting," Erica said. "Care to tell me her end of the conversation?"

"It appears the dragon recognized Ciara. It must be a friend or relative. It begged Ciara to help them," Brenn told her.

Ciara flew them to his home without further incident, but Brenn thought it rather interesting that high up above them was a small black speck. It was as if the black dragon was watching over them.

CHAPTER SIX

Ivran, Laro, and Aldis, had not yet returned when Ciara landed in the courtyard, and as they slid down, Brenn noticed no hovercraft. He was concerned. Collecting the venom was hazardous, as were the blister plants.

"Brenn, you're back. We found what you wanted," Tomas shouted as he and Erica entered through the back door into the kitchen to find Tomas and Shanina munching away on a bowl of fruit.

Brenn glanced at the timepiece hanging on the wall of the kitchen. "I want to get the formula and ingredients to our science building before sundown. I wonder what is keeping the others. I hope they didn't meet with danger. I'm hungry. Let's have a bite to eat, Erica, while we wait."

One of the kitchen aides quickly placed a platter of fresh bread and slabs of meat on the table and filled two goblets with wine.

"It amazes me. Your technology is so far advanced, yet many of your customs are almost medieval according to Earth standards. It's a delightful mix," Erica told him.

"Please sit. One day, when everything is behind us, I would like to learn more about Earth, its customs, and the fairy tales you speak of. I am also sure our king would like to learn why your planet is dying, so we can avoid making the same mistakes on Ierilia. I must compliment you on picking

38

up our language so fast. I notice you barely using your translator."

"Brenn, I have a tendency to pick up languages. I speak quite a few, all of them on Earth of course, so you would not have heard of them, but I learned them merely by visiting the different countries. Mm, this tastes like ham."

"Ham?"

"Pork meat. Pig meat. I don't know if you have any animals like it here. All of your food is like a feast to us because food on Earth has become so scarce. Only the very wealthy can afford to buy meats and fish. Our oceans and rivers are polluted. The only fish available are cultured in special science buildings, the same with fruits and vegetables. There are very few farm animals left or bird species. People on Earth are allotted special protein bars to try and save the population."

"Yet you have tasted this ham on Earth? You were wealthy?" Brenn asked.

"No. Because we were all being sent out to space to prepare a colony on another planet, our government prepared a farewell feast for us. At the feast, I ate foods I'd never tasted in my life. Ham was one of them."

"May the gods and goddesses prevent such disaster ever befalls Ierilia," Brenn muttered as he drank his wine, then held his goblet up for a refill.

Just then, Ivran, Laro, and Aldis came into the kitchen. They looked a little the worse for wear, Laro minus his tunic. Aldis produced two vials from his bag and held them up triumphantly.

"Venom!"

Laro held up a small container. "Blister plants!"

Ivran sported an arm bound with what looked like strips of what used to be Laro's tunic.

Brenn jumped off his chair. "Ivran, are you all right?"

One of the kitchen staff was already busy unwrapping Ivran's arm. Brenn gasped when he saw the huge blisters on Ivran's skin.

A drop of my tears will heal them. Use them. I can give you more tears if necessary.

Brenn hesitantly took out the vial that contained Ciara's tears. Carefully, he dripped a couple of drops onto Ivran's blisters. They shriveled instantly. "How did that happen?" he asked.

"I tripped and fell, my arm hitting one of the plants. What did you just put on my arm? The pain is gone, and the blisters have dried up."

"Ciara's tears."

"I should have guessed. You have to be careful that no one finds out about the power of her tears."

"I know, but I need you whole. As soon as our scientists make the potion, we will depart in our attempt to retrieve Cewrick's son. I know you must be hungry. There is plenty to eat," Brenn said as he motioned for the new arrivals to take a seat at the table.

Laro, Ivran, and Aldis seated themselves. The kitchen staff brought out three more glasses of wine as well as more platters of meat, bread, and fruit.

"Erica, how is it that you are here?" Laro asked.

"King Biryn has allowed me to assist. I knew something odd was happening when the weather went crazy. Then the next morning, those awful black creatures took Mark and Laura," Erica said, her voice wavering. "I couldn't stand by and do nothing. I have to get them back."

"How were they taken? I would have expected your crew to be indoors with their instructors, learning the language and about our planet's customs," Aldis said, then took a sip of wine.

"Mark loves the outdoors and horses. He was just coming

in from the stables when one of those black dragons plucked him from the ground. Laura was sitting out on the verandah, and the same thing happened. It all happened so quickly. I still hear Laura's screams in my head."

"I am sorry about your people, Erica. We will find a way to save them and the others that were taken. We had many taken as well, including children. Cewrick does not discriminate to get what he wants," Brenn said while helping himself to more bread.

"King Biryn told me why Cewrick has done this. We would have gladly helped you rescue your people. Earth had many factions, not unlike Cewrick and his minions. These factions coveted what they did not have and did not care who they killed or hurt to gain it, even going as far as destroying the very thing they were trying to take. It's one of the reasons my planet was ruined," Erica explained as she wiped tears from her eyes.

Brenn watched as Laro reached out to grasp Erica's hand in his. He could see the worry in his friend's eyes as he looked at the strong woman before him. "We will stop Cewrick before anything like that ever happens here."

After they had their fill of the food, Brenn collected the ingredients for the potion and placed them into a pack for Aldis. "We need these taken to the science building quickly. We leave when the suns rise if they have the formula ready."

Aldis took the pack from Brenn and left with Erica to deliver the ingredients and the formula.

Everyone had retired for the night, but Brenn was restless, waiting for news about the potion. The formula seemed quite simple, but scientists were finicky and would want to test the ingredients first.

His communicator finally buzzed. "Brenn, the potion is almost finished. I just spoke with Als Gnuak, head of the laboratories, and they have produced five flasks of potion," Aldis informed him.

"Five?"

"We will each carry a flask, in case we run into trouble and we lose a flask or break them."

"Good plan."

"They are just now testing each flask to be sure everything is in order, as they made several batches. When I hear back from them that the potion is good to go, I will contact you. Be ready to leave at sunup."

"Have you decided to involve any of your officers for this mission, Aldis?"

"There are a few more of us now. I have contacted five of my most trusted officers, one of them is a medic, and I gave them the option. They have agreed to go with us. I have also arranged for weapons, climbing gear, glimmer sticks, and provisions. All of us will have to carry a large pack. Going to the center of the planet will take just a little bit longer than one day."

Brenn chuckled. "You think? Going to the center, much of it will be descending. Coming back is going to be a lot more difficult. And who knows what we will find along the way, or what will find us."

"One moment. Als is contacting me on the official channel."

Brenn waited, but not long.

"The potion is approved. Get a good night's rest. We're leaving at first light tomorrow."

"Will you contact Erica?"

"Yes. She'll be with me. You can inform Ivran and Laro to be ready. I will pick the three of you up."

Brenn hurried to Ivran and Laro's rooms and softly knocked on their doors. They both stuck their heads out at the same time. "We leave at sunup. Aldis just contacted me. Be up early. I will have suitable clothing and gear for you in front of your doors. Bring your bedroll."

Brenn returned to his quarters, where he dug up his space-fleet clothes. They would fit Ivran and Laro as they were similar in size. He also put a warm leather jacket on each pile. It was going to be damp and cold in the tunnels. After he placed the clothing and gear in front of their doors, he went back to his rooms. All he wanted now was to spend just a bit of time with his lifemate.

Ciara was already waiting for him in his bed. He quickly took his clothes off and joined her. "That was quite an adventure today, Ciara," he said as he took her into his arms.

"It was. Tomorrow, you begin the biggest adventure of your life, and I wish I could be with you. All I can do is give you my tears in case any of you are wounded. Before you sleep, fetch a small flask."

"That's not hard. I have a flask right here, next to my bed. You will stay with me tonight?"

"Yes, my love. But only to hold you. You need to rest. This quest is going to be difficult and fraught with danger. You have no idea of the creatures that lurk beneath the planet's crust."

"We will have weapons, and there will be ten of us," Brenn said while nuzzling her neck.

"One of the five men chosen by Aldis cannot be trusted. He is a follower of Cewrick."

"How do you know? Who is it?" Brenn asked.

"I do not know which one. Be very careful. He will try to kill you all to stop you from reaching Cewrick's son."

"And you know this how? And how does Cewrick even know of our plans to give this man orders?"

"Brenn, why do you question me? If only I had my full powers. I would be able to do so much more."

He answered her by kissing her nose, her cheeks, nibbling

at her ear.

"Stop it," she softly admonished him. "You will not be able to contain your lust. Wait until you are back. For now, let us just lie quietly in each other's arms."

"But who knows if I'll make it back?" Brenn murmured against her lips.

"You will, my love. Now sleep," she whispered, then kissed him. "I will be watching over your loved ones and waiting for you here."

Unwillingly, he felt himself drift off, sure that she had placed a sleep spell on him, but he couldn't fight it.

Brenn woke up well before sunup. To his disappointment, Ciara had left his bed. He understood. She had wanted him to rest well before their difficult mission. The flask lay beside his pillow. He picked it up and put it inside his bedroll. He hoped he wouldn't have to use her tears—that no one would be hurt—but from what Ciara had said, there were dangerous creatures lurking below. That thought caused him to glance at his sword. Yes, they would have fleet weapons, but he would feel better carrying his trusted friend that had been at his side through many a battle.

He'd left messages for the kitchen staff the night before to have breakfast ready early. So after he bathed and dressed, he hurried to Ivran and Laro's rooms to wake them.

Like him, they were up, dressed and ready to go. "Have you said your farewells?" he asked them both.

"Yes," Ivran said, and Laro nodded.

"Good. The kitchen staff should have a hearty breakfast ready for us. Do you have your bedrolls? Your jackets I left for you?" Brenn glanced at their attire. The suits fit them well, but they weren't wearing the jackets.

They hurriedly went back into their rooms to fetch them. Brenn sighed. He hoped it wasn't a mistake to take them along. They were not experienced in any kind of warfare, and who knew what they would encounter beneath Ierilia's crust. After they joined him, this time carrying their bedroll and jacket, he led the way to the kitchens.

"This will be the last hearty meal until we return. We cannot carry food with us," he warned.

"How will we survive?" Laro asked while spreading a chunk of warm bread with butoro.

"We'll be eating space rations. They're small enough to carry in our packs. There should be plenty of drinkable water available in the tunnels."

"Sounds appetizing," Ivran commented. "Give me a slab of this meat anytime."

"You can still change your minds," Brenn said while he helped himself to the eggs the staff had placed on the table. He glanced at the window and saw the sky brightening. "Hurry up and eat. Aldis will be here soon to pick us up."

After they finished their breakfast, Brenn led the way into the courtyard to the landing pad. In the distance, he saw Ciara in his orchard.

The sky turned a brilliant red, and within minutes, the suns began to rise, and Aldis and Erica arrived. Brenn, Laro, and Ivran hurried to the hovercraft.

"Your packs are all in the back," Aldis told them.

"Where are your five officers?" Brenn wondered.

"They are flying directly to the cave entrance. We will meet them there. Why do you have your sword? You're not going into ground battle."

"It might come in handy. Who knows what we will find down there. Give me the vials. I must take them to Ciara quickly so she can cast her spell upon the potion."

Aldis reached inside the craft and handed them over. Brenn took them and hurried to the orchard to Ciara.

He placed them on the ground in front of her and gasped

as Ciara's body began to glow with a silvery-purple light that surrounded the vials. Within moments the light flared a bright purple, then disappeared.

It is done. Take them, you must hurry.

Brenn picked up the vials of the now bespelled potion and placed them carefully in the bag. "Goodbye, my siren," Brenn said as he reached out to touch her graceful neck.

Farewell, my love. Until we meet again. May the goddess of strength, Tarphine, be with you.

CHAPTER SEVEN

After everyone was seated in the hovercraft, Brenn watched as Aldis punched the coordinates of the cave into the console. "One of your officers is a spy for Cewrick. We must be on the lookout for a trap."

"How could you possibly know this? I chose five of my best, most trusted people. My three lieutenants are genetically engineered. You know the program. You, yourself, have several units in your legion made up of them. There is no way they could possibly be working for Cewrick." Aldis turned to Brenn, giving him a shocked look after setting the hovercraft to autopilot.

"Ciara told me. She senses when things are going to happen. I trust her implicitly. She has been right each time she has given me a warning." Brenn pinned Aldis with a hard stare. "She could not tell me which of the five it could be, but with the knowledge that your lieutenants are from the Auris Project, we need to focus on your other two team members, the captains."

"You two are speaking in riddles now. Please explain?" Erica commented behind him.

"The Auris Project was started during the reign of King Tyrol the third, King Biryn's grandfather several generations removed. Long ago, Ierilia was a warring planet, each realm fighting the other until the population of Ierilia was almost decimated. King Tyrol took control of the planet and started the genetic engineering project to help produce soldiers to protect the realms and bring peace to the planet."

"Wow. So what happened on Earth almost happened here. If only we would have had so much knowledge. Then again, our realms, or as we call them, nations, possibly would have stolen such a project and with all of them having genetically engineered soldiers, war could have gone on forever. Your realm is the only one with such knowledge?"

"Yes, it is. The building is well hidden and heavily protected."

"What if Cewrick has spies planted there as well?" Erica asked.

"The scientists that work inside the building have no access to the outside world. They committed themselves to the project and gave up their right to live among us. They live within the complex in a small world of their own. Some even have families, the children growing up within the walls, although they are allowed no more than one offspring. The children are kept away from the laboratories. When they reach puberty, they are given the choice to stay with their parents and train to work there, or to leave and be placed with family members. Some choose to stay and receive training, while others leave to live with grandparents or other family. The secrets of the Auris Project can never leave those walls. No one goes in or out of the gates. When a group of soldiers has been created and trained, they are fetched by one of our stealth hovercrafts during the night and quickly transported to our army barracks," Aldis said.

"We need to be on the alert and watch your two captains closely," Brenn told him.

"I agree. I don't have time to research which one it could be. At least we know that our mission is compromised. We will take every precaution to keep everyone safe."

"It is good that each of us will carry a vial of the potion. Cewrick's minion may try to destroy it. Only we know there are five vials," Brenn said.

"That was a good idea in case we get separated for any reason, or the potion is discovered by the spy," Ivran said.

The hovercraft slowed down, then came to a stop. They had reached the mouth of the caves. "We will watch each other's backs. I will not lose any of you on this trip."

"Look outside. My team is already waiting. Nothing looks amiss," Aldis said, and he powered the hovercraft down and opened the door.

"Looks can be deceiving, and I trust the dragon," Erica said. "She saved my crew twice. I will not doubt her words now."

Brenn handed each of them a vial of the potion. "Keep it safe. We do not know what lies ahead."

They grabbed their packs and weapons and disembarked from the hovercraft. Brenn took his sword and placed it in the sheath strapped to his back, then followed Aldis to the team that had arrived earlier, while Laro, Ivran, and Erica fetched the rest of the gear and caught up with them.

Aldis pointed to each of his team. "This is Captains Dour and Arval and Lieutenants Dunmore, Garnoc, and Trevain." Aldis addressed his men. "You, of course, know who the general is. Our other teammates are Laro, Ivran, and Erica."

Brenn gave them a hard stare. "I am leading this mission. You are here to assist us in getting to the bowels of the planet. Your lives and ours depend on you following my orders."

He could feel fear coming from two of the officers, a little overpowering at first. He was still trying to get used to the lion's advanced senses. Maybe he could use that to his advantage and ferret out exactly who the traitor in the group was. He didn't like the idea of their backs being to any of the five. "We will start into the cave paired up. Dour and Garnoc take the lead, Trevain and Dunmore next, Aldis and Arval, Laro and Erica, Ivran and I will take the rear. Be on the lookout for kurakeldas. They will be abundant in these caves."

Brenn followed the group into the cave, holding a glimmer stick in one hand and his weapon ready in the other. He glanced over at Ivran, who was doing the same. He didn't sense fear from Ivran but a fierce determination. Brenn could feel the lion in Ivran, could sense the agony of the lion at being caged, of not being able to make a connection to the human. Was it like that for all of them? Brenn focused on Laro and felt the same determination but also a fierce need to protect, the same need he felt to protect Ciara.

Ciara's soul shard warmed against his chest. He didn't need it to summon her after the spell that bound her to the Clyss was broken, but he knew a piece of her human soul resided in it. It made him feel safer that he carried a small piece of her close to his heart.

Brenn pulled himself out of his musings and looked forward. Every instinct he had warned him of danger ahead. Ciara's soul shard burned his skin through the leather pouch that contained it. "There is danger ahead. Be ready for it," he said through the mouthpiece of his headset.

Ahead, Brenn could see the tunnel opening up into a huge cavern. The sound of legs scuttling along the walls echoed within it.

"Kurakeldas! A whole nest of them!" Dour, the first one to enter the cavern, yelled as he fired his weapon at the huge spiders, disturbing the nest.

"Move quickly!" Aldis shouted. "We cannot fight them in pairs. It is going to take all of us to kill them now that they're scattered."

Brenn fired his weapon on a kurakelda that was scurrying across the rock ceiling above them. They were lucky it was a nest of babies. He didn't think the ten of them could handle so many adults.

Weapons fired all around him as he made his way into the cavern with the others. It felt as if they were shooting at the spiders for hours until the last one fell, but he knew they weren't finished. Somewhere in these caves was the mother, and by the size of that nest, she had to be huge.

"Garnoc! Dunmore! Burn the nest," Brenn said. He turned to look at his other team members while Garnoc and Dunmore set the nest on fire. "Check the walls and the ceiling. We need to make sure this cavern is clear."

"Everything is clear," Aldis said.

"I hate spiders!" Erica exclaimed, and a shudder ran through her body. "Those are gigantic! You didn't say anything about huge fucking spiders!" she shrieked as she punched Laro in the shoulder.

"We need to keep a watch out for the mother. That was a nest of babies," Brenn said, then looked at Erica. "They are kurakeldas, not fucking. I have never heard of this fucking spider. Are they from Earth?"

"What do you mean those were babies? Are you telling me you have gargantuan fucking spiders and we just killed all of its young?"

"They are kurakeldas. You have the same spiders on Earth, but you call them gargantuan fucking?" Brenn questioned her again.

Erica burst out laughing. "No, we don't have these on Earth."

"I do not think this situation is funny, Erica," Laro said.

"I'm sorry. I apologize." Erica was still giggling. "It's the language difference. *Fucking* is a cuss word."

"Cuss word?" Laro asked.

"A word that's used when angry, in a bad situation, or when frustrated. Strangely enough, it's also a word for sexual activity, or during it," Erica explained.

"That makes no sense," Brenn said.

"This is hardly the place to explain it all fully," Erica told him. "After this mission, I'll tell you more. Just be prepared, you may hear me utter the word on occasion, and it won't be meant sexually."

"Sexually means what?"

"Sex means two people being intimate. And that's all I'm going to tell you, because I'm looking at the most gigantic motherfucker spider in the universe," Erica shouted and fired upon it. It disintegrated, only a small pile of dust remaining.

"I am not even going to question that word." Brenn grunted. "You reacted fast, Erica. Let us continue to the other side of the cavern."

Erica walked next to Brenn as they continued. "Brenn, I'm amazed by the genetically engineered soldiers. They don't look or sound any different from us," she said softly so the others couldn't hear.

"I know. They appear human, but they are not. Many of their internal organs are mechanical, enabling them to breathe where we would have to use our oxygen. They also do not feel heat or cold and have no human feelings, so would not hesitate to kill a friend if necessary."

Erica sighed. "They can't be killed?"

"Yes. They are not invulnerable. But upon death, no one will grieve for them," Brenn told her.

"Rather sad, really. They also don't talk much, I've noticed," Erica said.

They entered another tunnel, descending quite fast. The ground was slippery from water that seeped down the walls steadily. Their glimmer sticks lit up the tunnel brightly. Small creatures scurried into crevasses as the group progressed.

They came to an abyss, as if an underground quake had split the ground in two. It was wide.

"Holy fuck," Erica exclaimed.

"Oh, now fuck is holy as well?" Laro asked.

"Told you I'd be using that word more than once. How do we get across? That's a hell of a far stretch," she wondered, obviously trying to contain her mirth at Laro's question.

"There is a stone crossing further down," Dour called out.

They headed for what looked like a ton of fallen rocks and boulders, creating a crossing to the other side. A loud sound came from inside the abyss. Brenn stopped, as did the others. They held their glimmer sticks down inside its depth but didn't see anything. Another loud growl.

"Hurry. Let's get to the other side," Brenn shouted.

"Be careful. The rocks are slippery," Aldis warned.

They had to climb over several of the large boulders and were almost across without incident when suddenly a huge head surfaced from the abyss. It was the most grotesque monster Brenn had ever seen. Its maw gaped open, displaying only rows and rows of spiked teeth. Its head was like a big round ball and covered in green slime. Beady white eyes glared at the group. A long white line shot out of its mouth, circling around Erica's waist. It lifted her off the rock.

"Holy fucking mother of god! Help me!" Erica screeched.

Brenn reacted instantly. He drew his sword and hacked at the line, cutting it off. The creature roared. Erica fell back into Laro's waiting arms.

"Run!" Brenn bellowed.

Laro was desperately trying to remove what appeared to be a very thin tongue, but tough as ore, from Erica's waist. Brenn helped him quickly. "Am I glad I decided to take my sword along," he muttered.

"Hurry! We must finish crossing!" Aldis yelled.

They ran, crossing to the other side, as the head of the monster lifted back out of the abyss, searching for the morsel it lost. What was left of its tongue dripped black-colored blood onto the rocks below. Its huge body undulated up and down along the wide divide in the cave's floor.

Brenn turned to see Dour raising his weapon to shoot the monster. "No! We are here to retrieve a huge worm-like creature. This may be what we're seeking."

"It can't be that easy," Laro said. "It is supposed to be in the bowels of the planet. We are not even close yet."

"I don't see us easily pouring anything down its throat, much less bring it with us," Erica said.

"I say we continue our journey. If this creature is the one we seek, we can come back to it," Aldis suggested.

Brenn nodded in agreement. "Agreed. I have no doubt we will come across this monster again. Let's continue. It's getting late, and we should find an area where we can rest relatively safely."

"Let's move out," Aldis said as he took the lead with Dour.

Brenn waited for the group to move forward and followed them, taking the rear with Ivran.

"Something bothers me about Dour," Ivran whispered to him. "I may just be looking for it. He would have destroyed the creature in the abyss if you hadn't stopped him. I also think he is the one that shot the nest of kurakeldas, knowing they would scatter and possibly wound or kill any one of us."

"I don't think Cewrick's spy would make it so obvious. We can't prove he was the one who stirred the kurakeldas, but I trust your instincts. We will watch both captains closely. Cewrick's spy is bound to make a mistake."

"I think we should post two watches at least while we rest. I don't think we should allow either of them to take watch alone."

They continued walking in silence. Ahead, Brenn could hear water dripping. The tunnel they had taken had a slight decline and started widening. Soon they reached the opening of a huge cavern. The beauty of it was stunning. Stalactites hung from the ceiling above a clear pool of water. Tall stalagmites rose gracefully to meet them. On the right of the tunnel, a stream of water flowed steadily into the pool of water below it. The water then flowed in a stream from the pool, cutting through the flat, smooth rock of the cavern floor.

"Secure the cavern. We will camp here for the night. Dunmore, test the water to ensure it is safe to drink," Brenn said.

Brenn walked to a section of the cavern that was relatively dry and the rock smooth enough for them to lay bedrolls out. The walls of the cavern had several sections indented that were large enough to fit a couple of bedrolls. He would ensure Erica had one alone for privacy.

A scream echoed across the cavern. Brenn looked up to see Dunmore staggering toward Aldis, holding a bleeding hand in his fist. Brenn grabbed the first aid kit and canteen from his pack and hurried toward them.

"Dunmore, let me see your hand," Aldis said.

Brenn could see that Dunmore had lost three of his fingers. "Here, rinse it off with some water." Brenn handed Aldis the canteen. "We'll bandage it quickly. Make sure he is given an extra protein bar at dinner. It will help restore his energy while his hand regenerates."

"What happened?" Aldis asked.

"I was testing the water as the general requested. A large fish leaped up and tore off three of my fingers." Dunmore looked at Brenn. "The water is drinkable, Sir, but we should collect it from the shallow stream and not the pool."

"Thank you, Dunmore. You may set up your bedroll and rest while your hand heals."

"Now I've seen everything," Erica commented. "Not only are they genetically engineered, but they regenerate? Unbelievable."

"His hand will regenerate overnight. A complete limb

takes quite a bit longer," Brenn told her. He watched Laro assist Erica in placing her bedroll, and it amused him to see Laro place his own next to hers. Laro saw him watching, so he quickly busied himself with his own bedroll.

"I cannot let her sleep alone. She is, after all, a female," Laro told Brenn.

"Uh-huh." Brenn grinned.

Brenn glanced at the couple and saw Erica turn to Laro, green eyes ablaze. "I might be a female, but I'm as fucking good as any of you. Don't you ever dare insult me like that again."

"There is that word again. I fail to see the relevance of this expression. It seems to apply to anything," Brenn muttered. "Ivran and Dour are taking the first watch. I take the next watch with Trevain, so I'm turning in. Goodnight, everyone. May we all rest in peace."

It was as if he had a built-in alarm. Brenn woke up right on time to take his turn to be on watch. He was surprised he had slept so soundly and had fallen asleep right away. Then again, their trek was difficult and taxing on the body. He quickly went to relieve himself behind a stalagmite, then joined Trevain, who had already released the other two from duty.

Brenn sat and leaned against the cave wall, his sword by his side.

"Why do you carry such a primitive weapon?" Trevain asked.

"Trevain, I am normally a ground soldier. You should know we don't use fleet weapons on the ground."

"Yes, General. But we're using fleet weapons for this mission."

"So we are. I like my sword," Brenn said.

The hours were going to be long, as he knew a conversation with Trevain would be very limited. Brenn thought about Ciara, remembering their magical night together. The shard felt warm against his chest as if she could read his mind. But he knew she couldn't. They had already descended too far. He fought to gain control over his longing for her. It was not the time or place to get distracted.

CHAPTER EIGHT

Aldis blew a whistle, waking everyone. Brenn stood and stretched. He'd had trouble staying awake. Thank the gods the night had been uneventful.

"It should be sunup up above. Time for us to eat and continue." Aldis raised his voice so they would all hear him.

The team hurriedly packed up their bedrolls. After discreetly relieving themselves, freshening up at the shallow end of the stream, they ate an energy bar, drank their allotment of water, and were ready to go.

At the far end of the cave were three entrances to tunnels. Aldis took out a map. "According to this, we need to take the center tunnel. Brenn and Ivran, you take the lead this time."

It didn't take long for the tunnel to become so narrow they had to walk sideways to fit through. Green slime dripped steadily down its walls.

"This stuff is gross," Brenn heard Erica say.

"Gross?" Laro asked her.

"Disgusting. Slimy. It stinks. And by the looks of those cute fishies in the stream, I doubt if we can bathe anywhere down here."

"Trust a woman to think of bathing at a time like this," Laro said. "Ouch. Why did you punch me?"

"You asked for it."

Brenn's laughter bellowed. He couldn't contain his mirth.

Laro might be smitten by the captain, but she was not a force to be reckoned with. He would have his hands full with such a strong-willed woman.

He came to a dead halt when all he saw was a wall in front of him with a narrow gap at the bottom. It hardly looked large enough for someone to roll through. Kneeling, he held his glimmer stick close. They would have to slide through on their backs.

"What is holding us up, Brenn?" Aldis shouted from behind.

"A wall. We have to slide through a narrow opening at the bottom, and I don't see an end. We may need to use our oxygen masks. I will go first." He took his oxygen mask out of his pack and put it on.

Gingerly, he laid on his back and, head first, began to slide into the opening. His usual terror of confined spaces attacked him, but he fought to control it. *What if a creature attacked in this narrow and shallow space?* There was no way they could fight back. By the gods, he could barely reach for his weapons. He heard his sword scrape the stone floor beneath him. Using both hands to propel himself through, it seemed to take a lifetime before he finally tumbled into another cavern. He rolled down and came to rest against a stalagmite. Holding his glimmer stick up, he waited as one by one the others appeared.

They all held up their glimmer sticks to see where they were. The cavern was ten times as large as the previous. Rose-colored stalagmites and stalactites were abundant. It was a sight of beauty to behold.

Brenn noticed Erica with a device in her hand. "What are you doing, Erica?"

"I'm taking pictures."

"Oh. An ancient method of memorizing places or events," Brenn surmised.

"Ancient to you, perhaps. But it's all I've got," she retorted.

"Aldis has been recording much of our journey. You will be able to view the holographic pictures after our return," Brenn told her.

"I've never seen such beauty in my life," she murmured. "As long as there aren't any fucking spiders here."

"Erica, please stop it with this fucking."

She giggled. "I am not fucking right now. I don't participate in voyeurism."

Brenn shook his head helplessly. "Never mind. Aldis, how are we for time?"

"This is our next rest stop. We have traveled for two days now, and we are already far into the evening. It is time to set up camp and rest for the night. Let us explore the cavern," Aldis told them.

They found a lake, again, crystal clear.

"Drinkable," Dunmore told them after testing the water.

The lake had a beach made up of tiny pebbles, fine enough that they could sit on it.

"If only I could bathe," Erica said, running her hands over her slime-covered uniform.

The water was so clear Brenn could see the bottom of the pool. "I don't see anything moving down there. This water is like ice, though," he said while swirling it with his hand.

"I don't care how cold it is. I just want to feel clean," Erica said as she tested the water for herself. "It's not too bad."

Brenn shook his head at her and laughed. "You go ahead and bathe if that's what you wish."

"We have skin suits in our packs that will radiate heat as soon as the material touches your body," Aldis said as he grabbed a small package out of his pack and handed it to her.

Erica opened the package and held up the infant-sized suit in her hand and gave them an arched stare. "I am supposed to fit myself in this tiny scrap of material? You are kidding, right?"

Laro grabbed one end of it and pulled. "See... it stretches. Even I know that, and I'm just a horse trader."

"And just how in the hell is this sliver of thin material supposed to warm me up?"

"You have strange words. What is this *hell?*" Brenn asked her.

"It's where we are headed to get that damn worm, but you still didn't tell me how this is supposed to warm me up. Tell me before I set foot in that icy water," Erica snapped, glaring at Brenn.

"As soon as the material makes contact with your skin, it causes a thermal reaction. It will begin heating, and you will be warm in seconds," Laro told her as he let go of the material and it snapped back into place.

"I'm trusting that you're telling me the truth." Erica grimaced as she dropped her pack and started pulling off her boots. "I can't wait to get this damn slime off me."

"You can wash with your clothing on to remove the slime, and we'll dry them with one of our fleet weapons using the wind blast setting." Brenn grinned at Erica. "We'll get camp set up. You worry about getting that *damn* slime off. It is pretty disgusting."

"Go to hell, Brenn." Erica laughed as she threw a boot at him.

"I think you've already established that we are rapidly on our way."

Brenn followed the others to set up their camp. The fine pebbles on the floor of the cavern would be much softer than the hard rock from the night before. He noticed that Laro set his bedroll next to Erica's again, taking care to make sure her bedroll was positioned against the cavern wall.

After setting up his bedroll, Brenn sat with Ivran and Laro on the pebbled beach. Erica had just finished washing and walked onto the beach, her teeth chattering and her lips blue from the icy water.

"You need to remove your wet battle suit, Erica," Laro told her as he held up a blanket to give her some privacy. "We can dry them for you, but you need to get into the skin suit swiftly."

Brenn grabbed the blanket from Laro. "Help her. Ivran and I will hold the blanket up to shield her."

Draping a blanket around her to hide her nakedness, Laro managed to assist Erica out of her wet battle suit, then helped her to put on the skin suit. Within seconds, her shivering stopped, and her lips turned back to their normal rose color.

"Holy fuck! I am not changing back into that battle suit." Erica pinned Brenn with a stare. "Is there a reason I can't wear this under my suit? It's as cold as the arctic down here, and this suit is amazingly warm."

"Arctic? A place on Earth? I wouldn't suggest keeping it on for too long, not unless you'd like to become as crispy as burned roasted bread. I'll dry your battle suit as quickly as I can."

"The arctic is all ice and snow. The cold is extreme. Don't you have snow and ice on Ierilia?" she asked.

"Yes, we do. Our winters can be quite harsh in some regions."

Brenn and Ivran quickly dried Erica's clothing while Laro helped her clean the slime off her boots. The fleet weapons were powerful and dried the suit and some of her strange items of clothing in less than ten minutes. Brenn took the clothing from where he had hung it between two stalagmites. He held up a wispy string with a triangular patch and wondered what it was. He was about to ask her but thought better of it. Some strange Earth attire, he guessed. The other item was obviously to support her breasts.

He glanced at her and could see a sheen of perspiration

already covering Erica's face and her cheeks starting to turn a bright shade of red. Brenn handed the dry clothing to Laro. "Ivran and I will hold up the blanket again while you help her change."

"It is late. We need to stop talking and bed down," Aldis called out. "Ivran and Arval have first watch. Laro and Garnoc will take the second watch. May the gods protect us this night."

Brenn looked forward to a full night of rest. According to their instruments, they had traveled quite a distance, but they had a long way to go. He doubted Cewrick's son would be in the center of Ierilia. According to scientists, the center was incredibly hot, and they would begin to encounter that heat soon, especially if they could start using their propulsion packs. He doubted that anything could live there and withstand the intense temperature.

Was the strange creature that popped up out of the abyss Cewrick's son? He doubted it. If Cewrick cursed his son to the bowels of the planet, he would have sent him to the hot core and the son would be dead. He wished he could talk to Ciara. She could have some answers for him. Alas, that was not possible.

Still thinking about the mystery of it all, he drifted off into a deep sleep.

Loud voices awakened him rudely. Grabbing his sword, he jumped up to see the group surrounded by a wall of glistening ice, caging them in. "What is this?" he demanded.

Aldis held up his hand. "Magick is at play here. Somehow, Cewrick knows we are down here looking for his son, and he knows exactly where we are."

"He is a powerful sorcerer," Brenn muttered, hacking at the ice with his sword. "What time is it?"

"Almost time for us to move on. What concerns me is how

does Cewrick know exactly where we are?"

"Now what?" Erica said.

"Not to worry. Our weapons can cut through that ice easily," Brenn told her.

"Okay. This sorcerer of yours scares the living shit out of me," she retorted.

Brenn ignored the strange expression and headed to Aldis, who had motioned to join him. They walked away from the group and spoke softly. "What do you think, Brenn?" Aldis said.

"One of the captains is somehow in contact with Cewrick. How else does he know where we are and where we are going?"

"I agree. But which of the two? Until we have solid proof, there is nothing we can do."

Brenn nodded. "For now, we will just blame it on Cewrick's powers. We need to melt through that ice. It will delay us somewhat, but our weapons are powerful."

"Everyone, aim your weapons at this spot all at once. We should be able to melt a large enough hole for us to get out of this cage," Brenn called out and joined the others, followed by Aldis. They formed a line.

"Ready?" Aldis asked. "On the count of three, fire."

They fired in unison. It took several attempts before the ice began to crumble and melt under the onslaught of the intense heat. Once the hole was big enough for them to crawl through, they gathered their gear and one by one left the ice cage.

"If that son of a bitch can do this, what else can happen?" Erica said. "Your dragon can't communicate with you down here. How come he can?"

"Ciara does not have her full powers to command. Until the curse is lifted from her, her magick is limited," Brenn explained.

"Do what you need to do. Eat something quickly. Drink plenty of water. We may as well continue now that we were so rudely awakened," Brenn told the group.

He quickly found a stalagmite to hide behind while he emptied his bladder, then hurried back and dug in his pack for a protein bar. While munching on it, he joined Aldis. "I was thinking last night. We cannot travel to the center of the planet. Have you thought about that? It would take us a very long time, plus we would never get close enough. The heat is too intense. What Cewrick called the bowels probably means somewhere in these tunnels and caves, not the core of the planet."

Aldis smiled. "Of course. I am not stupid, Brenn. We've traveled two days so far. The farther we go, the warmer it will get. I have a feeling we will find our little worm soon."

"Sorry. We did not discuss it in enough detail. Before we find him, we need to ferret out the traitor. Let us continue. I will take the lead."

At the far end of the cavern, they found a tunnel. Brenn shone his glimmer stick inside and noticed its very steep decline. "We are going to have to slide down this one. It is too steep to walk. It feels wet and slimy, so we should be able to descend easily," he called out to the others.

"Oh, fucking fantastic. More slime. Just what I need," Erica muttered.

"I will lead." Brenn stepped into the tunnel and sat, then pushed off on the walls. He had not expected to barrel down so fast. It was like sitting in one of the carnival attractions, except this took much longer. He could barely hold on to his glimmer stick as he slid. It seemed to go on forever, and at times it was so steep he feared falling forward. Wondering what would happen at the end of it, he closed his eyes and continued to slither. He could feel it getting much warmer. That meant they were getting closer to the core. After he opened his eyes, the glimmer stick showed him the exit, but he hardly had time to react and try to brace himself. He attempted to grab the walls, but it was no use. They were too slimy, and his hands just slipped. Reaching the end, he plunged over the edge and held his breath. Right into a pool of water. Unlike the other pools, this water was tepid. Sputtering, he surfaced to see his team surfacing near him.

He held his glimmer stick above the water. They had landed in another huge cavern. "Swim to the edge," he shouted. "We don't know what lurks below."

They all swam to the edge of the pool and stepped onto another beach, this one of fine silvery sand. Strangely enough, plants were growing in the background. Weird-looking plants, some resembled trees and, from what Brenn could see, even some strange colorful flowers.

"What worries me is how the fuck will we ever get back up?" Erica said as she lay panting on the sand.

Sticking their glimmer sticks in the sand to light up the area, they looked around.

"It is a crystal cave," Brenn said.

"It's breathtaking," Erica commented while taking her pictures. "Fuck. My battery just died."

"It is also quite hot here. At the rate the temperature is rising, we can't go too much further," Aldis told them.

"The boy cannot be far from here," Ivran said.

"Who knows how much heat the worm can withstand?" Brenn wondered.

Still panting, Erica told them, "After that roller coaster ride, I think I need to rest for a bit. This seems like a futile mission. The worm could be much farther down, and we can't travel too much further, or we'll be roasted chickens."

They sat in little groups as they drank their water and had something to eat. Ivran, Brenn, Laro, and Erica sat together.

"I do not think we are going to find the son, Brenn," Ivran

commented.

"It will not be for lack of trying. My worry is the same as Erica's. How to get back up from where we came," he answered and frowned.

"Yes. There is no Ciara to help us here," Laro added.

Erica stood and walked to the edge of the water. "I'm going to go for a swim to get the slime off my suit," she said and promptly walked into the pool, ignoring the warnings from the men that there could be unfriendly fish lurking beneath its inviting appearance.

She was up to her waist when suddenly the water began to swirl, and a gigantic worm-like creature rose above its surface. It had dozens of little arms, a flat head, and a forked tongue that slithered in and out of its mouth. Its girth was the size of a yewnettle tree. It was so big its head almost reached the cave's roof.

Erica left the pool fast and fell onto the sand. "Fuck!"

Beady eyes surveyed the group on the sand. Weapons ready, they waited to see what the beast would do.

Was this Cewrick's son, Brenn wondered, never taking his eyes off the creature. Suddenly he noticed a heavy gold chain with an amulet attached to it dangling from one of the scales on the worm's neck. Yes, it had to be the son. Unless the creature had killed the worm, because the thing was so big, it hardly resembled a worm, except it was round.

The amulet depicted an image of the goddess Rania and a baby's face, but it was broken, half of it missing. A pale glow radiated from it, the stone shimmering in hues of blue and green. From the corner of his eyes, he saw Captain Arval set his weapon on kill. "Arval. It has not attacked us. This could be the son. Do not kill!" he ordered.

"All of you, stay where you are. I will kill anyone that moves," the captain said, his lips a grim line.

Aldis tried to stand, but Arval immediately fired right next to the admiral. "I said do not move."

"So, you are the traitor among us," Aldis said softly.

"The son will overpower the father. This cannot happen. Cewrick will be a great leader on our planet. My orders are to stop you from releasing him, to kill him," Arval shouted.

"I am ordering you to stand down," Aldis responded. "You have been a trusted officer in my fleet for a long time. What happened?"

"Cewrick's reign will be supreme. I will be admiral, and you will be gone. You and your team can rot down here."

"You were caged in with us when Cewrick made the ice cage. You were ready to die for him?" Ivran yelled.

"He would have saved me."

Brenn saw Arval bend and take something out of his pack. It was a round silver disc with a bright red stone in its center. The heavy silver edge had strange symbols etched into it. Arval activated it somehow, and a bright red glow appeared above the disc. "I await your orders, master," he said.

A loud raspy voice came from the device. "You found him?"

"Yes, master."

"Kill him. I will now place a curse on those wretched individuals that would attempt to overthrow me by releasing the whelp that fell from that stupid woman's loins."

Brenn watched in horror as the icon began to hum. The voice chanted the first word of a curse.

The worm was still watching them. Arval had his back to it and did not notice its advancing head. Its mouth opened to reveal sharp fangs. In less than a second, the creature grabbed Arval and killed him. The disc fell from Arval's hand into the water, shooting sparks as it hit the surface. The chanting ceased, and the red glow faded to black as it drifted to the bottom of the pool. The worm shook the slain body of the captain clamped in its jaws, then flung it to the far end of the cavern. It hit the wall with a sickening *thud*, its mangled flesh splattering blood, and guts tumbling to the rock floor below.

Holding his breath, Brenn watched the creature. It merely observed them, did not try to attack. Was this the son? He stood and approached the edge of the pool. "Can you understand me? Are you Cewrick's son?" he asked, his hand on his weapon, ready for an attack.

Of course the creature could not answer him. It gazed at Brenn for a few moments, then slid back into the pool. Brenn turned around. "Strange. I could have sworn it knew what was happening. At least now we know who the traitor was in our midst."

The worm-like creature surfaced again. Brenn heard the water's turmoil and swiveled. Its head came toward him, its beady eyes focused on the small human on the sand. Brenn stood his ground, ready to act. It did not attack him. "We are here to rescue you. If you are Cewrick's son, can you give us a sign that you understand? That you are the son?"

Its head approached closer to Brenn. He stepped back, but the creature's head followed him. It did not lash out, did not attempt to snatch him, so Brenn stood firm, although his hand was still on his weapon. "You must be the son, or you would have tried to kill me. I have a potion that will return you to your natural state. Will you let me pour it into your mouth?"

The creature's mouth opened wide, displaying its teeth and tongue, but it did not move.

"Okay, everyone, give me your vials. I never expected it to be this big. It might need all of the potion to bring it back to its human body," he called out to the others.

Ivran, Laro, Erica, and Aldis quickly brought their vials to him.

"Are you sure of this, Brenn?" Aldis asked.

"I think it is him. Did you not notice the amulet hanging on a scale near its neck? It could have killed me easily, but it did not. Yet it killed Arval when he threatened us, and just in time, too, because the sorcerer was about to curse us to this place for eternity." He opened the vials and, one by one, poured the liquid into the creature's mouth.

They watched as it convulsed, turning the water of the pool into a churning vortex. Bright lights flashed around the writhing body of the creature, causing the water to glow in hues of many different colors, then faded as quickly as they had appeared.

Brenn stepped back a few paces and waited, his teammates behind him.

"Maybe the potion's dosage was too big, and it killed him," Erica pointed out. "The vortex is calming, and there's no sign of anything."

"Wait. Look," Brenn said and pointed.

A figure materialized within the pool, surfacing and spluttering. A naked man walked out of the water and stood before them. His black, tangled, wild hair hung to his waist. He had a beard down to his chest. As tall as Brenn, he stood watching them, feeling his body, then his face, in wonder. Long, slim fingers examined every contour of his face, then tugged at the long beard.

"By the gods, it is him," Laro said.

The man balled his fist and hit his chest. "I am Icaras, son of Cewrick and Hirsuta. I am his son no longer. From this day forth, I am only Hirsuta's son. I am forever in your debt for releasing me from my captivity. Why did you rescue me? Cewrick is hated by the people on Ierilia, so they would hate his son."

"We came to remove your curse and enlist your help in defeating Cewrick," Brenn said as he gave the wet man a blanket to wrap around himself. "We have clothing for you and the means to cut your hair and shave, if you wish."

"Please, I would like to. This very long hair feels strange,

70

and I did not have hair on my face when Cewrick placed this curse on me." Icaras took the blanket from Brenn and covered himself.

"How old were you when this happened?" Laro asked.

"I was fifteen years old. I don't know how old I am now. I lost count of the time I have been trapped."

Aldis turned and faced the team. "Start setting up camp here. We need to take the time to rest well before undertaking the grueling journey back to the surface."

Brenn retrieved a battle suit, boots, and a toiletry kit from one of the packs and gave them to Icaras. "The suit should fit you. I hope the boots will. I have a knife you can use to cut some of your hair and beard away."

"Thank you." Icaras took the clothing and dressed quickly. "I have never cut my own hair. I am not sure how to do it."

Brenn motioned for Icaras to sit down on a rock. Carefully he cut Icaras' hair until it was shoulder length, then handed the knife to him.

Brenn wondered if Icaras knew how to shave. The boy was only fifteen when he had been rudely removed from his home, and more than likely had not yet begun to grow a beard.

Icaras took the sharp blade from Brenn and used the water as a looking glass to shear off the long beard and mustache. Then he carefully scraped the whiskers off his cheeks. Icaras turned and grinned in satisfaction. "I remember watching my uncle doing this," he told Brenn.

"Here, let me brush your hair for you," Erica offered, approaching with a small brush.

Brenn watched Erica struggle with the tangled hair, Icaras pulling faces as she wrestled with knots. He had never been face to face with Cewrick, but he had seen holograms of the sorcerer. He would recognize those silver-gray eyes anywhere. He was indeed Cewrick's son. The gold chain and amulet now visible after the beard was gone also proved it. The eyes were where the resemblance to Cewrick ended. Icaras' smile was one of pure innocence. His dark hair curled around his shoulders in waves. He had a strong jaw. Dimples dotted both cheeks, and he had a cleft in his strong chin. His demeanor was that of a young adolescent, and he looked to be a man in his late twenties, though he could be centuries old. He was as tall as Brenn, with a large muscular build like he practiced daily with a sword. He could easily pass for one of Brenn's soldiers. He had never seen an image of the mother, but he guessed Icaras looked like her. Fortunate for him.

After Erica finished brushing the man's hair, Brenn placed a hand on Icaras' shoulder. "Come, I imagine you are hungry. We brought an extra bedroll and pack for your use."

Brenn, Erica, and Icaras joined the others where they had set up camp. Aldis passed a protein bar to them and introduced everyone to Icaras.

Erica sat opposite Icaras. "Whoa! What a difference a cut and a shave makes."

Icaras looked down shyly. "The last time I saw my reflection I was fifteen. I knew I would look older, but to actually see myself now as a man is quite a shock."

"I can imagine it was," Aldis said as he passed a canteen to Icaras.

"That is a beautiful pendant. What does the symbol stand for?" Erica asked.

As Icaras touched the pendant around his neck, a pained look crossed his face. "My mother placed it around my neck when I was born. It was given to her by the goddess Rania, but a piece of it is missing. If you look at the back, it seems that there was another part to it, as if it was once two-sided. I used to wonder about that when I was a boy."

"Does anyone have an idea of how we are going to get back up that tunnel?" Ivran asked. "Now that we have found

Icaras, I am rather anxious to find a way back out of here."

"We have climbing gear, but it will not be easy to scale the tunnel with such a steep incline and how slippery the rocks are. We slid down at super speed. Going back up will take a very long time," Brenn said, then took a bite from his protein bar. "We do not have the room to place handholds into the rock, and with how slimy it is, if one person above missteps, we will all come tumbling down."

"I can lead you from this cavern to the surface. I know several ways out of here," Icaras told them.

"I would have thought Cewrick would have kept you trapped as far down as possible. His magic works down here. We had firsthand experience," Aldis said.

"Once Cewrick cursed me and cast me out, he was no longer concerned that I would grow into my powers, because I would not be able to use them. He did not watch the caverns. I could travel through them as far as that huge worm body would allow me, though I could never return to the surface. Cewrick created a barrier that stopped me from advancing too close."

"Cewrick will set traps for us. If not down here, they will be there when we near the surface. We will have to be prepared. He will not allow Icaras to go free if he can stop it," Brenn said.

Icaras looked at Brenn. "I may not know how to control my powers yet, but I do have my own magick to use against Cewrick."

Brenn could sense the power radiating from Icaras. It was unnoticeable when the curse was first lifted. But it was growing too quickly and could possibly pose a danger to all of them. He hoped Icaras had had enough training in his youth that would help him contain and control the force that was being unleashed within.

They sat in a circle, except for the three lieutenants. They rarely interacted with their teammates. From what Brenn had learned about genetically engineered soldiers, they had little or no emotions.

They all munched on small strips of dried and salted kurakeldas. "We know your father placed the curse on you because he learned your magick would be stronger than his when coming into your full powers," Brenn said, looking at Icaras.

"My powers began to surface just before I had my fifteenth birthday. My uncle, Cewrick's brother, told him. Uncle Geven did not realize the hatred my father felt for me and that the knowledge that my magick would be immensely more powerful than his would cause his wrath. Uncle Geven paid with his life for trusting Cewrick.

"Please, do not ever call him my father again. That day, Cewrick summoned me. I was still naive and lived in the hope that Cewrick would recognize me as his son and love me instead of the hatred I felt radiating from him."

Erica shook her head with a look of confusion. "Why did he hate you so? After all, he didn't know about your magick until then."

"I think because I look so much like my mother. I do not know the story behind Cewrick and my mother, and why he made her his mate, because he seemed to hate her, too."

"Why didn't he kill you?" Erica wondered.

"I do not know. Perhaps he thought I would be subservient like all his other subjects. When I was thirteen, I began to display some rebellion that he did not like. Then to learn that soon my powers would be ten times as great as his, if not more, angered him beyond belief. After he summoned me, he vented his wrath and told me he'd killed my uncle for lying to him all those years. He yelled a lot about my mother and I feared for her well-being. I was terrified but did not know how to defend myself against him. Why he did not kill me

74

then is still a mystery and will probably always remain as such. It saddens me deeply to learn he also killed my mother. She was a good woman."

"You didn't know?" Ciara asked.

"No. I only knew he had killed Uncle Geven. This angered me. My uncle was more father to me than Cewrick. I hardly had the chance to confront him about it. He placed the curse on me and I found myself here."

Brenn needed to get Icaras to Ciara as quickly as possible. She would know how to help and how to train the man to control his magick. "Enough conversation for now. We can talk a lot more when we return to the surface. Let's get some rest. We will have a full day of trying to escape this cavern in the morning. I will take first watch. I don't see a point in two of us standing watch now. Icaras took care of our traitor for us."

CHAPTER NINE

Brenn woke to the sounds of talking. He was surprised he had slept so soundly and that the others were awake before him. He rubbed his face with his hands and left his bedroll, relieved himself behind a rock, then walked to the pool of water and quickly washed his face and hands. Looking up, he noticed the group sitting in a semicircle facing the pool of water, watching Icaras. Mesmerized, he stopped to watch him before joining the group.

Icaras knelt by the pool, swirling his hands under the water. The surface glowed like there was a fire beneath its depths, while large white fish leaped out of the water and landed on the bank beside him. Brenn was amazed at the power radiating from Icaras in such a short time. *How formidable will he be when he comes into his full power?* Brenn shook his head, walked to the group, and sat down.

"Just look at him. He is hot as hell! He can put his shoes under my bed anytime." Erica giggled.

"Hot? What do you mean? Why would he put his shoes under your bed? You say so many strange things," Brenn said.

Laro glared at Erica. "I think I know what this *hot* and *shoes* mean. I do not like some of your strange words."

Erica took Laro's hand in hers. "Are you jealous? You have no reason to be! As far as I know, we are not a couple!"

"Yes, we are!" Laro growled low in his throat.

Brenn snapped his head up and looked at Laro in surprise. It sounded almost as if the lion had come to the surface. In shock, he watched as Laro grabbed Erica by the shoulders and pulled her against his chest. Then he captured her lips in a passionate kiss. That was so unlike Laro. He was usually easygoing and shy with women. Brenn noticed Erica was stiff as a board in Laro's arms. He was almost ready to break them apart until he saw her relax against Laro, obviously enjoying the kiss. Brenn shook his head at them. Then Laro pulled back, kissed Erica's lips one more time, and looked down at her. He was even more surprised at Laro's next words.

"You are mine."

"Now wait a minute there, bucko," Erica said, glaring at Laro. "Just because you kissed me doesn't mean we are a thing!"

Brenn chuckled as Erica stalked off and started packing up her bedroll and supplies. Even more amused, he watched Laro follow quickly behind her. Ivran joined Brenn in laughter as they watched Laro's retreating back.

"You can't just tell a strong woman like Erica that she is yours," Ivran said, shaking his head and laughing. "Reana would have skinned me alive."

Icaras joined them with several fish he'd cleaned by the water. "I do not care for your protein bars," he said, smiling at them. "I have caught enough for everyone if you would like one? They aren't bad. I have survived by eating these uncooked and other creatures that live within these caverns."

Icaras placed the fish on a large rock he had cleaned with some water. Then he passed his hand over the fish, fire blazing down from his fingertips. Soon, the mouthwatering scent of the cooking fish filled the air. "After so many days of protein bars and water, these fish will be a feast."

Brenn took a bite of the fish Icaras had given him and

looked over the group. Laro and Erica had rejoined them while Icaras cooked. "We must hurry and eat. It would be best to get to the surface as quick as possible."

"What other passages are there out of this cavern? I have searched everywhere. The only way out I could find is the tunnel we fell through," Aldis said.

"We swim out," Icaras told them.

"What do you mean we swim out?" Erica covered her mouth as she gasped. "Through the pool? That water is really deep. We will drown!"

Aldis took a drink of water from his canteen. "There are breathing masks in our packs in preparation for diminishing oxygen in the tunnels. They will sustain us while we swim."

Icaras looked at Aldis. "This pool is fed by a spring from a cavern above. It is a long way to swim up. We will have to swim down under a large portion of rock, then through a tunnel to the next cavern. Will your masks sustain you for that long of a swim? If not, I might be able to place a spell on you, enabling you to breathe underwater."

"Yes, they should last. The masks are designed to provide forty-eight hours of oxygen with normal breathing before they need to be recharged, and there are small chargers in our packs and a replacement oxygen cell. No spells necessary," Aldis said.

Brenn took another bite of his fish, enjoying the taste of the fresh meat even if it lacked spices. "Cut that time in half to be safe. We must consider the exertion of swimming with our packs."

"How will we swim with our packs? Everything will get soaked. Wet blankets are heavy. Won't it weigh us down?" Erica asked.

"We are trained to swim underwater with full packs and gear, and the packs are waterproof. One of us will carry your pack for you," Brenn told her as he went to finish packing his gear.

The group finished their breakfast, then grabbed their packs to join the three lieutenants waiting by the edge of the pool with their breathing masks already on.

Brenn pulled his mask out of his pack. The mask was lightweight with a light attached to the forehead and self-oxygenating. It fit over the head and created an airtight seal around the neck of the person wearing it. It was equipped with internal communicators to allow them to keep in contact and a button on the side by the mouth that when pushed would activate the oxygen. The fleet used them in low-or no-oxygen situations.

Brenn showed Laro, Ivran, and Erica how to wear the mask and activate the oxygen before donning his own. It had been a long time since he had been required to use one, and he hated the restrictive feel of it around his neck. It reminded him of his official uniform. "We are ready."

"Stay close to me while we are under the water. There are creatures in the depths that would make a meal of you," Icaras warned them, then dived into the water. One by one the group followed.

Brenn was the last to dive in. He was a strong swimmer and quickly caught up to the rest of the group. The light from his breathing mask illuminated the water around him. He could easily see Ivran and Laro up ahead. Every now and then, he glanced behind him. Icaras would protect them by leading, but what could attack from the rear was what worried him.

The tunnel they swam through was dark and dismal. Lack of any light prohibited anything from growing under the waters except algae and strange-looking fish, none of which seemed interested in the humans invading their territory.

The tunnel seemed long, very long.

A bright flash lit up the water. "What's going on?" Brenn

spoke into his com.

"A school of missile fish. They have a very long spike and can penetrate their prey in less than a second after which they devour their catch. I sent them all to a different pool in the caves. No need to kill them," Icaras replied.

"Remind me never to get on his bad side," Erica muttered.

Brenn grinned. She obviously forgot they could all hear each other.

"All of you have my eternal gratitude. I swear a solemn oath I will never harm you. Or anyone outside Cewrick's castle. We have arrived at the upward tunnel. When all of us are inside the tunnel, I will create a vortex that will start behind Brenn, pushing us all up very fast.".

"This sure as fucking hell beats walking," Erica said.

"Give me walking anytime," Brenn answered, his claustrophobia attacking after he'd entered the narrow vertical tunnel. He felt the water churning behind him—a tremendous push as it surged upward, taking him and those above him with it. He sped upward so fast that his ears whistled and his head throbbed. He surfaced to see his team swimming to the edge of a translucent pool.

For a moment, getting his bearings and allowing the dizziness to settle, he glanced around. They were in a huge, spectacular cavern. It was so breathtakingly beautiful it was almost indescribable. The whole cavern was crystal. The crystals were everywhere he looked, protruding from the ceiling and scattered on the cavern floor, which also seemed to be pure crystal. The crystals were a myriad of all the colors of the rainbow, sparkling, sending reflections to the surface of the pool. The expanse looked as if it was lit by dozens of torches, yet Brenn saw none.

When he turned around, he saw a crystal island in the center. On it stood a miniature crystal castle, big enough for a child to play in. *Who could have made this sculpture?* It was magnificently carved.

"Brenn, are you going to stay in the water, or are you joining us?" Ivran called.

He swam to the shore that consisted of the pearliest beach he had ever seen. The sand was super fine and warm. After removing his oxygen mask, he said, "Did you all see the island in the center? The castle?"

"We're not blind, Brenn," Erica snapped. "Of course we've seen it. It's breathtaking. Gorgeous."

"Who could have crafted it?" Laro wondered.

They did not have to wonder too long. After they made camp and sat talking, Aldis cried out. "Look at the castle!"

The castle had lit up, sending brilliant light throughout the cave.

"Something that beautiful cannot be Cewrick's doing," Laro said.

"I agree. Look, something came out of it and is watching us," Ivran said while pointing.

A figure the size of a six-year-old child stood gazing at them. Brenn dug his distance surveyor out of his pack and held it to his eyes. He saw a miniature woman. Her skin was glittery gold, and her hair was a bright, shiny gold that hung to her ankles. She wore a flimsy wrap-around piece of material that also sparkled with the same colors as the crystals. Six gossamer wings protruded from her back. He tried to draw the image in closer, but couldn't.

"It is a fairy," Erica muttered. "A real fairy."

"I do not know what a fairy is, but she is truly magical," Dour said.

The apparition rose slowly, hovered above the castle for a few moments, then rapidly flew toward them. Magical or not, Brenn had his weapon ready. It could be a Cewrick trick.

She landed at the edge of the pool. Brenn studied her features. Large slanted eyes, also a myriad of colors, gazed at them, studying the group. Her gaze finally settled on Icaras. She walked toward him and stopped.

"Icaras. I have been waiting for you for a very long time. You will release me from the spell your father placed on me and on my priestesses."

"How? Who are you? I have been to this pool before and never saw the castle or you," Icaras said.

"I am Niqine, high priestess of the Chihni priestesses. We are the goddess Rania's handmaidens, placed on Ierilia to guard the book of knowledge and the icon that will complete your magical powers. You were not to see us until the time was right."

"How are you here?" Icaras inquired of her.

"Your father, Cewrick, coveted the sacred book of knowledge and the icon that was only to be placed in your hands. He captured my priestesses, but I escaped with the book and the icon to this magical cave created by the goddess Rania. Cewrick placed a spell on me that trapped me to this place."

"How did you get here? You are so fragile and dainty. How could you traverse the tunnels?" Brenn asked.

"The goddess used her powers."

"Why could the goddess not release you from the cave?" Icaras asked. "I thought she was all-powerful."

"She is. I do not know why she could not release me. Maybe she chose not to. I do know Cewrick has no knowledge of the creation of this cave. Rania kept me protected from him, and I have protected the icon and the book."

"I cannot imagine that the goddess could not overpower Cewrick's spell. I would think she chose not to release you. Where is this book? Can we see it?" Icaras asked.

"The book is in the castle. It contains all the knowledge of the past, present, and the future."

"Who enters this knowledge into the book?" Icaras asked.

"The book is older than time and was created by the gods. All knowledge is entered automatically. It only permits us to see what we are allowed to know. I will go and fetch the icon so that you may come into your full magical powers, Icaras."

They watched her whiz away back to her castle. She soon returned, carrying a glass cage. She set it before Icaras and told him, "Open it."

"How? Do I break the glass?"

"Touch it."

Icaras reached out carefully and placed his hand on the box. Instantly it sprung open. He reached inside and produced a small exquisitely carved golden statue of a goddess, a wand in one tiny hand, a torch in the other. Brenn watched as Icaras gazed at it. Then, suddenly, his eyes rolled back in his head. His body convulsed several times. Raising his arms high, the statue above his head in both hands now, he called out the goddess' name.

"Rania. Rania."

Lightning came out of nowhere. They all had to shield their eyes. Brenn peeked and saw the lightning strike Icaras again and again.

A melodious voice echoed throughout the cavern. "Icaras, my child, my beloved grandson, you have released my handmaidens from Cewrick's spell. You now have your full magick, but you must learn how to use it wisely. After you return to the surface, Ciara will be your teacher, and Niqine will also guide you. Ciara's magick is as powerful as yours. Niqine, my priestess, your magick is released, too, and the spell removed. Your handmaidens reside in the Tideless Abyss. They are safe. After I freed them from Cewrick, I sent them to the Tideless Abyss to keep them protected. I have shielded both the mountains and this cave from Cewrick's magick and minions. He cannot enter them. Niqine, Icaras can view the book of knowledge. I will allow Brenn to look upon it as well. I will provide him with the sight. Guide them into the castle. The book of knowledge must remain there, as always, only accessible to you and I. All of you will be protected when you make your escape from here."

The voice faded. Brenn looked at Icaras, who had collapsed onto the sand. He was still holding the statue and gazing at it in pure wonderment.

"That must have hurt like hell," Erica commented.

"What? I did not feel anything. What happened?" Icaras asked.

"Lightning bolts struck you, many of them, but your skin is not marked," Brenn told him.

Brenn suddenly felt as if the world was spinning out of control. Multicolored lights encased his body. Sparks and flares of light flew around him. His stomach was queasy, and he thought he was going to lose the fish he had eaten for breakfast. No sooner had the lights begun their dance around him, when they vanished just as fast. He found himself staring up at the members of his group. Shocked, he looked at Icaras, who was at eye-level with him.

"Whoa! That was fucking awesome!" Erica exclaimed. "Look at them both. They are now as tiny as Niqine!"

"Come, we must hurry. Rania awaits us," Niqine said as she held out her hands to Brenn and Icaras.

Brenn grasped Niqine's hand while Icaras took the other. He gasped as his feet left the floor of the cave. His body floated along with Niqine's as she guided them into the small castle.

The castle's interior was just as beautiful as its exterior, carved solely of crystal. The colorful, translucent walls were as smooth as glass. Brenn could see the shadows of his team waiting outside for him by the pool of water. In the center of the room was an altar cut of the same crystal as the castle. Placed on the altar was what appeared to be a crystal book.

Standing next to the altar was a crystalline figure of a beautiful woman. The statue appeared as translucent and colorful as the walls of the castle.

Brenn gasped in surprise as Niqine ran to the statue and kneeled before it so low her head touched the statue's feet. Brenn watched in shock as the sculpture seemed to come to life smiling down upon the tiny priestess.

"My Goddess," Niqine said as she rose to stand before a glowing woman.

"Child, you have done well as the guardian of the book and the icon. You may leave with Icaras, for he will need your guidance."

Brenn could not believe what he was seeing. Was this truly the goddess? How incredibly beautiful she was. How extremely fragile she looked. Her crystalline hair flowed over her shoulders and down to her feet in soft waves. She reached a delicate, glass-like hand out to Brenn. "Come to me, warrior."

Brenn could not help but come to her call. Standing before her, he felt the aura of power shifting around her in waves. This being was not as fragile as she looked. Brenn bowed his head and kneeled before the goddess Rania.

"I cannot spare you the pain of this, but it must be done for you to read the book and for you to be whole in both body and soul."

Rania placed her hand upon Brenn's head. That aura of power that surrounded the goddess engulfed him. It felt as if his skull would split apart. He couldn't help but cry out. The tendrils of pain shot from his skull into his body. Intense heat seared him from within, then radiated outward. The lion, caged for so long inside him, roared as the man screamed in agony, the fire within melding the two together until they were one. His body felt as if it would implode from the force of the joining. He groaned as his system shut down, collapsing to the floor, blissfully passing out before the goddess completed her task.

A cool hand touched the side of Brenn's face. He could barely open his eyes, and his body felt as if he had been ripped apart by a morcoug. *Just a little longer, warrior, and your pain will cease.* He sighed as her cooling touch sank into him, healing the ache within. He stood up carefully, testing his body to make sure the torture had truly passed. He felt so strange, his mind confused. What had just happened to him?

"You may now read the book of knowledge," Rania said as she motioned Brenn and Icaras to the altar.

Brenn gazed at the book the goddess pointed to. He was not sure if it actually could be called a book. It didn't resemble any book he'd seen before, much less an ancient one that had been written before time. It was made of crystal and appeared more like a tablet than a book. It resembled the castle, in that it was translucent and shining with a myriad of colors. The edges were etched with symbols that pulsed with color. The center looked as if it was etched with the book's name, but he couldn't be sure. A page turned, the etchings in the center fading.

Brenn stood transfixed as the book rose above the altar, lighting from within, as a fiery-looking finger seemed to imprint upon its glass-like surface. Images began to appear in a dizzying rush of war, treacherous, all-consuming, all-destroying. Lions and humans roaming a valley that looked much like his home. Jeweled dragons flew the sky above them as lion cubs played joyfully with children. A fiery image of a grotesque man, his wild hair like blazing fire, his face a mask of hate, looking down upon the valley below. Ciara in dragon form, running alongside a wounded sapphire-blue dragon. Cewrick looking down upon a young Icaras with intense hatred and rage. He slapped the boy across the mouth, causing his lip to split and bleed. Brenn taking his first steps as a toddler, his mother's sweet voice praising him in the background. Ciara, the night he had met her in the Clyss. His village attacked and destroyed. The images kept flying before Brenn's eyes. The very last image showed a young peasant woman gathering herbs. Long black hair hung to below her waist. She turned and seemed to gaze directly at them, her eyes a stormy silver-gray like Icaras' eyes. He wondered vaguely who she could be until the image faded and he saw their arrival into the cave of crystal. The images stopped. The book was once again lying upon the altar as if it had never been disturbed. Could that have been an image of Icaras' mother?

"I have provided you with what I can. It is time you left this cave and returned to the surface," Rania told them.

"Thank you, my goddess," Niqine said as she bowed her head to Rania.

Within moments, Brenn found himself transported back to his team, his body returning to its normal size. "I do not know how you all feel," he said, looking at Icaras, who had also returned to his normal height. "But after that ordeal, my stomach is telling me my body needs refueling."

Niqine stood close to them. "I am returning with you, but I can now make the journey much faster and easier. Especially with Icaras' help. Between the two of us, we can send the whole group to the surface in a second. Gather your supplies and packs, get ready, and stand close together." She beckoned Icaras to join her.

"I'll go for that. Beam me up, Scotty!" Erica said.

They hastily packed up whatever they had unpacked and stood close to each other. Niqine and Icaras joined hands, closed their eyes, and began to chant in a foreign tongue.

CHAPTER TEN

Looking bewildered, Erica gazed at the hovercraft and shook her head. "I still think I died in that crash. Beam me up, Scotty really worked! We're back. But I guarantee none of this is real."

Laro laughed. "I don't know what this beam me up, Scotty means. No, you're not dead, and it's not a dream."

"Something from a TV series on Earth," Erica muttered, obviously feeling foolish.

"What is TV or series?" Brenn asked.

"It's a flat screen on the wall, and it shows enactments of stories. A series is when it's continued every week or every day for an hour each time, with the same characters but different stories. What I just said is from *Star Trek,* a science-fiction series," she explained.

"I think we had such many, many years ago. Now, we can watch an enactment of a story in holographic images," he told her.

Aldis gave instructions to his four remaining officers to return to base, again emphasizing upon them that this was a highly classified mission. "Let us go to your house, Brenn. I am in dire need of a hearty meal."

"I think I'm more in dire need of a bath and then a meal," Erica said.

Laro grunted. "Can women think of anything else but a

bath?"

You have returned safely.

Brenn snapped to attention as Ciara spoke to him while he was directing Niqine and Icaras into the craft and helping them buckle up.

I will see you soon after they have all retired for the night.

"I will see you before then, Ciara. It appears Icaras is going to be your pupil, so I need to introduce him to you."

"Ciara is communicating with you?" Aldis asked.

"Yes. I am not in the habit of talking to myself," Brenn muttered.

Who decreed this?

"The goddess Rania. She spoke to us."

Did she appear to you?

"Yes, and it was a mesmerizing experience. I will tell you everything later. We are about to depart," he said while strapping himself into his seat, wondering why he had spoken aloud. Ciara could hear his thoughts, but speaking to her in his mind was still something he needed to get used to.

Aldis set the coordinates for Brenn's house and pushed the high-velocity button. In minutes, they arrived at his estate.

Ivran's mate flew into his arms. Shanina greeted Brenn the same way, while his parents watched from the verandah. Tomas merely smiled happily, glad that his father was home safe. "I think I might join your troops, Brenn," Laro commented. "To be greeted as you and Ivran just have been upon return is heartwarming."

"Ivran is not a warrior."

"Does his mate greet him like that all the time?" Laro asked.

"No. I am generally at home at work in my blacksmith shop," Ivran retorted, having overheard the exchange.

Brenn looked at Niqine and Icaras standing alone, looking lost.

"Shanina, this is Icaras, Cewrick's son. And this pretty little lady is Niqine, high priestess for the goddess Rania," Brenn introduced them. "You can look after them. Give Icaras clothing from my wardrobe, and show Niqine to a guest room. Then show them the baths. We will all gather in the dining room for a celebration meal in two hours."

Aldis approached Brenn. "I have changed my mind. I want to join my family. I will report to the king and head to my house, where my family anxiously awaits me. I may join you on future missions, Brenn. You have no idea how much I enjoyed this one. I might ask the king to demote me. I am tired of sitting in an office merely handing out orders and overseeing space missions. I am still young enough to be on active duty. The king can find an older high-ranking officer to take my place."

Brenn smiled. They clasped hands in the usual greeting and Aldis disappeared into his craft.

Erica was about to follow Aldis, then stopped and faced Brenn. "Can I stay at your house?"

"If you like. You're more than welcome. My house is large and has many rooms."

Brenn watched Aldis fly away before his gaze trained on the orchard. He saw Ciara beneath the trees. She was awake and gazing at him.

"Brenn, the little priestess is so endearing." Shanina interrupted the moment.

"She is, and quite magical. I need to bathe, sister. Please give the kitchen staff orders to have a feast prepared in two hours? We need to celebrate this one small victory over Cewrick."

"Small?" Shanina asked.

"Yes. The biggest is to come. To overthrow Cewrick. But now, with his son's help, we may succeed."

"He is so handsome." She sighed.

"And much too old for you, little sister. He might act like your age, but in reality, he has lived many years. Do not dream about anything more than friendship. I am warning you," Brenn told her in a strict tone.

"You are not my father."

"No, I am not. But our father would or will agree with me, should I tell him of your desires."

"You wouldn't dare." Shanina stomped her foot.

"Don't tempt me. Now go and do as I have told you." Brenn grinned as she hurried away. He could not blame his sister for being enamored of Cewrick's son. He was a man and could admire Icaras' beautiful features and body. He was indeed a stunning male. Brenn hoped Icaras would find a lifemate in the future, one that could guide him and keep him on the right path. He quickly headed for his house, followed by Erica.

After he had shown Erica to a guest room, he hurried to his quarters. He took his time bathing, feeling as if the slime from the tunnels was still stuck to his skin and in his hair. After dressing, he went to the dining room, where he already found most of his guests waiting and enjoying his wine. He sat and one of his staff hastened to fill his goblet.

Brenn lifted it high. "To a successful and interesting adventure," he toasted. He gazed at the people around his long dining table. What an interesting mix they were. He noticed that Niqine's wings had retracted. Now, he had the time to really study her. What a beautiful little specimen she was with her sparkling gold skin and her pure gold long hair. Her face was exquisite, absolute perfection, her tiny body the same.

His staff came in carrying platters of roasted meats and vegetables, the aroma making his stomach rumble so loud it caused a giggle from his sister.

"I think my brother is hungry," she said loudly, causing

laughter around the table.

Brenn could not help but see his sister's flirting looks at Icaras. How was he going to stop this infatuation she had developed in just a few hours?

My love, do not worry. I can help with your sister.

He tried to put the situation out of his mind and hungrily attacked the food that was served. Meat had never tasted so good, nor vegetables or bread. Never would he go on a space mission and have to live on what they provided for meals. No, he would remain a ground warrior. If he ran out of field rations, he could at least hunt or fish for meat and collect berries or fruit.

Brenn's thoughts turned to Niqine and what she had told them in the crystal cave. If the goddess Rania, all this time, had been unable to remove the curses placed on Icaras and Niqine, they had to be dealing with a stronger foe than Cewrick. Rania was the goddess of magick. Wouldn't her powers be stronger than Cewrick's? Could Cewrick have the help of some malevolent being? It was possible.

Rania chose not to release Niqine from the spell that trapped her for centuries. What could be the reason? After all, Rania had saved the handmaidens and placed them in the Tideless Abyss, so why did Niqine have to stay in the crystal cave? If something as simple as a potion returned Icaras to his rightful form, couldn't the same be used to free Ciara?

All these curses and magick made his head ache. He didn't even want to begin to think about the images the book of knowledge had shown him. Brenn took a deep drink from his wineglass to help dispel the dull throb in his head and returned his attention to celebrating with his friends and family.

"Come on, we still have time for a game before father chases me to bed," Tomas said as he grabbed Shanina's hand, dragging her to the door. Brenn smiled at their antics, then noticed Shanina wasn't as willing to go and play with Tomas that evening. Her attention was focused on Icaras. He heard her sigh as she gave in to Tomas. Brenn knew Shanina would never hurt the boy's feelings by turning down his request.

Shanina stopped, turned and smiled at Icaras. "Want to come and explore the orchard with us? It'll be fun."

Icaras' face lit with pleasure as he grinned back at Shanina.

"It has been so long since I have played," Icaras said as he left the table to join Shanina and Tomas. The three of them sped from the dining hall.

"Brenn, do you remember the legends of the little people I told you while you were young?" Yartah asked.

Brenn thought back to the stories his father had told of the little people. From what he remembered of the legends, the little people were tiny like Niqine but were the colors of the rainbow, not gold like the priestess. "I do not remember a lot of detail. Mainly their description. You stopped telling them to me when I was a young lad."

"You were more interested in stories of battles and war when you were older. That was what fueled your wish to join the king's guard."

Brenn grinned at Yartah. "Yes, war stories did interest me more than rainbow-colored, flying little people that spread happiness across the valley."

Niqine erupted in tinkling laughter. "Rainbow colored? I have heard many of the legends, but I have yet to hear that one. Yes, they were stories of the goddess' handmaidens, but over time the stories changed and were embellished until the handmaidens were unrecognizable."

"So you did fly around spreading joy across the land?" Erica giggled. "You are beginning to sound like one of Earth's fairy legends."

"No, we did not. As Rania's handmaidens, we spread magick across the land, creating mystical places like the Clyss

Valley. We are called the Chihni."

"Are there male Chihni? With how small and petite you are, I bet you have the tiniest babies," Erica said wistfully.

"No, the Chihni are only female. We were created by the goddess Rania to breathe magick into this world and protect the book of knowledge. We are ageless and have no desire for a mate, or have children as the Ierilians do."

"No mates... no babies... no desire... but how can you be happy? Do you not wish to procreate?" Erica wondered.

"We were created to serve the goddess and create the magick of this world. That is what brings us true joy. We have procreated in our own way."

Brenn smiled at Erica's questions. He had no doubt that once Laro and Erica did accept each other, their family would start quickly.

"Rania told us she sent your handmaidens to the Tideless Abyss, which we know was the home of the jewel dragons. Where did you live before that?"

"In the valley between the mountains near your home. The Chihni shared the valley and those mountains with your ancestors. I remember the lions roaming freely before Cewrick placed the curse on your pride and the jewel dragons. Cewrick's father, Jysim, was a powerful sorcerer but not at all like his son. Jysim used his magick sparingly. He was a good man. He and his mate, Abelle, often mingled with the people of Ierilia.

"There was talk whether Cewrick had poisoned his parents or caused their mysterious simultaneous deaths in some manner. Cewrick was very young when they died. He had barely begun to come into some of his powers. He was always a nasty, rebellious child. The goddess Rania suspected the boy had help, but how, or from who, she did not know. The book of knowledge did not tell us." Niqine sighed. "There was a time when all the people on the planet lived in peace and harmony. When jewel dragons were often seen flying toward our cities, towns, and markets. They would revert to their human once they reached their destination, buy their wares, and change back to their dragon, then carry their goods over the treacherous cliffs that are on this side of the Tideless Abyss."

Yartah nodded. "I remember my great-grandfather telling us such stories."

"What was his name?" Niqine asked.

"Orino," Yartah replied.

Niqine smiled. "I knew him well. He was a great man. He and his mate have gone to the realm of dreams?"

"Yes, as have my parents. I am now alpha," Yartah told her.

"What kind of help would Cewrick have had?" Erica asked.

"We do not know. Whatever or whoever has to be evil, a malevolent creature."

Brenn suddenly remembered something he had seen in the book of knowledge. "I saw a face, so ugly and vile it is indescribable, surrounded by a mass of fiery hair. I only saw it briefly. Who could this be?"

Niqine frowned. "I saw it, too. I will ask Rania about the image."

The evening flew by. Icaras, Shanina, and Tomas returned to the dining hall for a snack of fruit and cheese after their games in the courtyard. Enthralled, his parents, sister, Reana, and Tomas listened to the tale of the rescue—Brenn, Ivran, and Laro taking turns in the telling of it.

Brenn finally ended the evening. "It is late, far beyond your bedtime," he told Shanina and Tomas.

"Tell us more?" Shanina pleaded.

Brenn stayed firm. "Enough for tonight. I am sure Icaras would like the feel of a real bed. I would like to retire for the night, too. As exciting as our mission sounds, believe me, it was fraught with danger. It will be surprising if we do not have nightmares about the monstrous creatures we encountered. Then again, they were offset by our experience in the magical crystal cave. Goodnight, everyone."

Brenn stood and hastened to his rooms. Yes, he was tired, but more than anything, he longed for Ciara.

CHAPTER ELEVEN

Her sweet fragrance greeted him as soon as he stepped through the door. Knowing he would find her waiting for him in all her naked glory, he quickly stripped off his clothing and hurried to his bedroom. A sweet smile played on her lips, her luminous eyes inviting him, her hands beckoning.

He climbed onto the bed and drew her into his arms. Her skin was moist as if she'd just bathed.

"I am so relieved you are home," she whispered against his lips.

He kissed her briefly, the tip of her nose, nibbled on her earlobe, then slid off her onto his side. He stroked her body with sweet, gentle strokes while drinking in her beauty. "I can never get enough of just gazing at you," he murmured. "You are so beautiful, so perfect, more intoxicating than the most potent wine I have ever consumed."

Her hand stole to his cock. She began teasing him, drawing the skin back and forth, pressing on his erogenous spot between his cock and his sack, then tracing the throbbing veins to the tip. She tapped her finger softly on the hole, rubbing the pre-come around the head. "Do not make me wait, my love. I need you to fill me."

Brenn slid his fingers up and down her moist folds that were already wet from her juices. She was ready, his exquisite siren, more than ready, and if he did not take her soon, he would erupt in her hand. He slid back on top of her, and his cock found its home. He buried himself deep inside her, felt her hips lifting to meet his thrust. He bent down to her chest and sucked a pert nipple while his hand kneaded her other breast.

She moaned and flung her legs around his waist. "Take me, Brenn. I can't contain myself much longer. I have waited for this moment. I have been on fire for you, my fear for you heightening my desire."

She drove his lust to the absolute peak. He began to move within her hard and fast, Ciara meeting his thrusts. Leaning on both hands, he gazed into her fathomless eyes, saw her parted lips, her tongue slightly protruding.

"Now!" she whispered.

His body shuddered, convulsed, as he released within her. Sinking down on top of her, gathering her into his arms, he stayed inside her until their breathing calmed. He kissed her and rolled to lie by her side, his arm still cradling her.

She leaned on her side and lifted her head to look down at him, her hair cascading over his chest. "Now, my warrior, you can tell me everything."

"Where to start?" he murmured.

"From the time you entered the tunnels to your return. My thoughts and prayers were with you the whole time you were down there."

He began talking, now and then taking a breath and stopping to kiss her. "What we saw in the book of knowledge was more than interesting. What disturbed me was an image of an ugly, wild-looking man with a mane of fiery hair. His face was distorted with hatred, his eyes blazing. And there was also an image of a peasant girl. I have no idea why she appeared."

"It is as if you are describing Zohmes. He was banned from

the realm of the gods and sent to the underworld. He swore revenge against the gods and began creating havoc on Ierilia. As for the peasant girl, I don't know."

"Why was he banned?" Brenn asked.

"He disobeyed Izarus, who sits upon the throne and reigns over the realm of the gods and goddesses. Izarus is the god of love and all things that are good and fair. The legend is that Zohmes killed a human who was favored by Izarus. When Zohmes was sent to the underworld, he became insane, hatred and revenge consuming him."

"Why were we shown his image?"

"I have a feeling he is in league with Cewrick. It explains a lot."

"How are we supposed to fight a god?" Brenn had visions of a furious Zohmes waving a flaming sword.

"You now have Rania on your side and Niqine's help. And do not forget your dragon. Between us, we are a formidable force."

"Tomorrow you will meet Icaras. Rania told us he will be your pupil. You as the teacher, Niqine as his guidance counselor."

Ciara smiled. "I saw Icaras playing with your sister and Tomas. He still acts like a boy, though he is now a full-grown man."

"And my sister is quite enamored over him," Brenn said with a deep sigh.

"I know. I watched them at play. Do not worry. Icaras will learn fast, and he will tire of child's play. Your sister will soon see him as a man much too old for her."

"How are you going to teach Icaras when you can only appear in human form during the night?"

"My dragon can enter his mind, just like I can speak in your mind. After Icaras has rested and recovered from his centuries of confinement, you can bring him to the orchard, and I will begin teaching him what he needs to know."

"Then begins the task of overthrowing Cewrick," Brenn mused.

"With, as I suspect, Zohmes assisting him, it will not be an easy task. Cewrick's magick will have waned when Icaras came into his full powers, but Zohmes is a fierce adversary."

"Rania was able to release Niqine, keep the handmaidens safe in the Tideless Abyss. Why can she not release you from your curse?" Brenn asked.

"A curse is different from a spell. Niqine and her handmaidens were bespelled. The curse upon the jewel dragons will only disappear with Cewrick's downfall."

"Then what did she do to me if not break my curse? She did not just grant me the power to read the book. She changed my whole being."

Ciara ran her fingers through Brenn's hair and placed a kiss on his shoulder. "Oh, my love, Rania could not have done so if our souls had not touched. The curse was not broken. It was burned from your soul. If I had not made that small connection between you and your lion, you would not have survived it."

"At least you can be in my arms at night," he murmured and kissed her neck.

Ciara leaned over him and kissed him on the lips. "Goodnight, my love. Sleep well." She placed her hand on his forehead, and though he fought it, he could not stop his eyelids from closing.

"I hate it when she does that," Brenn muttered, waking up to find his arms and bed empty. But he saw the sunlight streaming in and knew she would have had to leave before the suns came up. He grimaced for a moment at the thought of her dragon emerging in his bedroom. She would rip the whole room apart and the floor and ceiling. Actually, half his house would be a pile of rubble. He sighed and wished for the time when he could love her day and night.

That time will come, my warrior.

"I hope sooner than later," he muttered as he hastened to freshen up and get dressed. He could hardly believe he'd slept so long.

When he entered the dining room, he saw the table laden with platters of food covered with silver domes. He thought everyone had already eaten, but soon, Laro, Erica, Ivran, Reana, and Niqine trickled in. "I see I am not the only one that slept late," Brenn said..

The kitchen staff brought in more platters. "Did everyone else already have breakfast?" Brenn asked.

"Yes, General. Your parents and the young ones already ate, including Icaras. Your parents are on the verandah. The young ones went to the orchard," Lorsan told him while he lifted the domes off the platters.

Brenn inhaled the aroma of freshly baked bread. Grabbing a chunk, he liberally spread it with butoro.

"If I live here long enough, I'll be the size of an elephant," Erica said.

"What is an elephant?" Laro inquired.

"An animal on Earth. Very large, very big all over," she told him while grimacing.

"That would not change my feelings for you," Laro murmured, but Brenn heard his comment and grinned.

"Brenn, what is our next mission?" Erica asked while helping herself to a large slab of smoked meat.

"Our mission?"

"You honestly don't think I'm going to sit on my backside, do you? I want to be part of taking down that god-awful sorcerer. Don't exclude me. Please," she said in a firm tone.

"I'll speak to the king. I can't make such decisions on my own," he told her.

"You're the general. Surely you can hire whoever you want for your troops?"

"Erica, you're a different case. You are not from our planet. Yes, I have to consult with the king. And no, no plans have been made yet to overthrow Cewrick."

"What difference does it make where I'm from? I have accepted the fact that we are stuck on Ierilia. It could have been a lot worse. We could have all died. Instead, we landed on a hospitable planet that can be a paradise once that evil guy is terminated."

"Erica, I need to consult with the goddess Rania, with Niqine, with Icaras."

"The team from Earth is destined to be part of Ierilia's future," Niqine said. "Erica will play a big part in helping to end Cewrick's reign of terror."

"There you go. The oracle has spoken," Erica muttered.

"Oracle?" Laro questioned.

"Oh, never mind," Erica snapped while glaring at Laro.

Brenn wondered how those two were ever going to get together. He could feel the vibrations between the two of them, but Erica seemed to be fighting her feelings. He wondered if she'd had a bad experience on Earth. Did she lose dear ones? Children? A husband?

"Erica, tell us about your life on Earth," he probed.

"What is there to tell? You already know our atmosphere was contaminated and that all life on Earth was threatened."

"Did you leave family behind?"

The expression of pain that fleetingly crossed her face did not escape him, nor Laro.

Laro reached out to take her hand. "If you do not want to talk about it, it's fine."

"I had a husband and a beautiful baby girl named Marina. We suffered extreme food deprivation. Rory caught a dangerous flu virus that he was unable to fight. His immune

102

system was shot. My baby died of the same flu. The vaccinations the government provided turned out to be too weak. I was already working for NASA, and when they asked for volunteers for the relocation missions, I was first in line. I'd been trained for such an event. Since I had nothing left to live for on Earth, I didn't care whether I lived or died." Her voice broke, and she angrily swiped at her eyes.

"I am so sorry," Brenn and Laro said almost in unison.

"What is NASA?" Ivran asked.

"It's short for National Aeronautics and Space Administration. It's a government space agency on Earth," she explained, quickly composing herself.

"You did not contract the disease?" Brenn asked.

"No. That was something else the government didn't tell us. NASA personnel received the full vaccinations, not the diluted versions. There wasn't enough for the population of the whole planet, and the flu reached epidemic proportions. Hundreds of thousands died from this flu."

Laro grasped her hand again. "I am so sorry. I have a child, so I can understand how devastating it must have been for you."

"Enough. Now tell me what's next?" Erica demanded to know. "I'm sure my crew is bored out of their minds. They wouldn't mind going on a mission of some kind."

"Erica, we are not just fighting Cewrick, but Ciara and I believe he has help from the god Zohmes. I have yet to find out how we can even begin to battle one of the gods, especially a fallen god like the one in the book of knowledge. At least Ciara thinks that it was an image of Zohmes when I described him to her."

"Then we should research! Does Ierilia not have a way to pass information down through the ages? Earth has libraries of books. The libraries contain knowledge of the past and present. If we needed information, we would research and find clues or possibly answers to our questions," Erica said.

"Of course we have places like these. The building your crew uses to learn our language houses the largest information center in the city." Brenn looked at Erica thoughtfully. Maybe that would satisfy her need to help and keep her out of trouble. "Would you be willing to do this research with a small team? Laro will assist you with the task as well as two of our analysts. I will contact Aldis and have them meet you at the information center."

Erica grinned at Brenn like an antuar with a bowl of cream. "Would you allow one of my crew members to assist? She is one of the best research technicians I have ever known. She specializes in historical data. Her younger sister, Laura, was taken by those creatures."

"I will allow it as long as this research technician can understand our language as well as you can."

Brenn turned to look at Ivran. "Do you remember the stories my father used to tell of the time before the dragons?"

"Of course I do. He used to scare the wits out of us with those stories when we got too unruly." Ivran chuckled.

"I am beginning to think some of those old stories of his may have some truth woven in them. Like the legends of the little people. While I take Icaras down to meet Ciara, have my father retell those stories and record them. Let us see what is truth and what is not," Brenn said. He stood up from the table and glanced back at Laro and Erica. "Any information you find on Zohmes, send it to my datapad. We will compare it all this evening." Then he left the dining hall to find Icaras in the orchard.

Brenn walked out to the courtyard, his communicator opened in one hand and Twink climbing up his other arm. "Aldis, I have sent Erica and Laro to the information center to research any data they can find on a fallen god named

Zohmes. Can you send a couple of your best analysts to assist them? Preferably from the Auris Project. We need people we can trust."

Aldis' voice came over the communicator. "I will send Dunmore and Trevain."

"Good choice. They are already privy to a lot of the information. They will know what to look for. Contact me after your meeting with the king," Brenn said as he closed his communicator.

Twink scampered the rest of the way up his arm to wrap around the back of his neck as he continued his walk to the orchard. The sound of laughter reached him as he caught sight of his sister, Tomas, and Icaras running through the trees, chasing each other. Twink perked up and scampered down his body to take off, running toward Shanina.

They are full of energy. You will not be able to contain Tomas and Shanina in the house this day. I have already summoned Icaras to join me in a little while for today's lessons. Let him play for now. He has missed much and will need to become an adult soon enough.

Her head bowed low and stopped near his chest. Brenn stroked the scales between her nostrils while gazing into her large purple eyes. "Even as a dragon, you are beyond beautiful, my siren," he said softly and placed a kiss on her nose.

"I saw that."

Icaras startled Brenn. "You two are going to be busy for some time. I have a meeting with the king after Aldis has met with him. Learn well, young man." He slapped Icaras on the shoulder and with a last glance at Ciara, left the orchard.

CHAPTER TWELVE

Biryn embraced Brenn. "I am so relieved that both of you survived this mission. Sit and tell me your version. Aldis was much too brief. He was anxious to go home to his family."

"Understandable. I think I would rather face an army than venture so deep underground ever again."

"Talking about armies. Aldis has resigned his commission as admiral, much to my disgust. He has requested a position either on the space fleet as commander of a ship or as commander of one of your legions. I cannot favor him and demote one of the fleet commanders, so I told him I would speak to you," the king told Brenn.

"We are not at war, so he will see little or no action on the ground at this time. But of course we need to defeat Cewrick and now perhaps another foe." He stroked his chin thoughtfully. "I could use a trusted commander, a man I can trust with my life. Aldis is such a man. Commander Zigeuner was killed in action during our last battle. I have not yet promoted any of my captains to take his place. I could offer this position to Aldis."

"So be it. Now tell me everything," Biryn asked while filling Brenn's goblet.

After Brenn finally stopped talking, Biryn said, "See, Aldis did not tell me all the details of the crystal palace and the book of knowledge. And Ciara thinks this image you saw was of the god Zohmes?"

"Yes, she does. Cewrick's magick might be waning because of Icaras' return, but if the sorcerer has Zohmes to assist him, he could still be very dangerous."

"But you now have the goddess Rania, Ciara, and what can Niqine do? And Icaras of course. Once Ciara has tutored him, he will be a formidable sorcerer."

Brenn nodded. "Yes. I am not sure if Niqine can do anything. She is very small and fragile and merely the keeper of the book of knowledge."

"Do you think she would like to meet with me?" Biryn asked.

"I'm sure she would. I'll ask her. Of course, you can issue a royal command," Brenn suggested.

"No. Just ask her."

Brenn looked at the large pendulum on the wall swinging back and forth. His stomach should have told him how long he'd been in the palace. It was close to dinner, and he'd had no lunch. They had been so busy talking that food was forgotten. "Biryn, I should head for home. It is getting late."

"I am so sorry. I have neglected my own duties in my eagerness to hear of your adventures. I had a council meeting I was supposed to attend. Alas, there is always tomorrow."

"When I know more, I will contact you," Brenn said and clasped arms with Biryn.

On his way home, Ciara contacted him.

Icaras is a fast learner. He has only just now gone to the house for dinner, and he is eager to resume lessons tomorrow. Brenn, the goddess Rania contacted me. Before you can begin the challenge to defeat Cewrick, you must complete several quests. The first involves entering the forbidden forest. And I was right in thinking the image you described was that of Zohmes. Rania confirmed it.

"Fighting a god is impossible," Brenn told her.

There is a way, but that is of later concern. Rania has the secret to defeating Cewrick. But it involves a very dangerous mission. First, you must go to the forbidden forest. Deep in the forest is a small house. It is guarded by dryons and black dragons. Within its walls is a sacred urn. You must fetch that urn. It is vital. Inside the urn are the ashes of the first sorcerer born unto Ierilia. Without Cewrick, Zohmes is still a formidable foe, but the god won't have Cewrick's magick to assist him. First, you need to defeat Cewrick. After the sorcerer is defeated, we can concentrate on Zohmes.

"No one has ever lived trying to enter that forest. You know that."

Icaras and I can place a spell around you and whoever accompanies you to protect you all from the curse placed upon the forest. I cannot tell you what you will find within. No one has lived to tell that tale.

"Will Icaras accompany us?"

No. At this time, he cannot be anywhere close to Cewrick's castle. You need to gather strong men, like the ones that accompanied you into the tunnels and caves.

"What does this urn do?"

I do not know. Rania will tell us after you bring it back.

He'd arrived home and quickly headed across the courtyard to the house. He stopped for a moment to glance at the orchard, but Ciara was well hidden from view. "Will I see you tonight, my love?"

You need to rest, Brenn. This will be a difficult journey. Begin arranging it when you are inside.

He gathered he would not be seeing her that night. Disappointed, he went inside and found everyone already seated in the dining room.

"The king kept you a long time," his mother said.

"Yes, he tends to do that. Ruling a world is a lonely task. It is time our king found himself a queen," Brenn said. "Evening all. Before I forget, Niqine, the king would really like to meet

108

you."

"I am honored. When?"

"He didn't say. I had to approach you first. I'll let him know, and I'm sure he'll send word."

Halfway through their meal, Brenn said, "Ivran, Laro, are you up for another mission? This one is very dangerous."

"Already?" Ivran asked.

"What is the mission," Laro demanded to know.

"This is only the first one. Rania called them quests. The first one involves entering the forbidden forest."

"No!" his mother yelled. "No one can enter that forest and live."

"Mother, calm down. Ciara and Icaras will bespell us so we can enter it without dropping dead." Brenn tried to reassure her. He saw Ivran's mate whispering to him and Tomas shaking his head wildly.

The boy jumped up. "No, Father, you cannot go. I only have you."

"I'll go with you, Brenn," Erica said quietly. "Action beats stuffy research."

"I will not pretend this isn't dangerous. We don't know what we will run across within the forest. We have to find a small house deep within that is guarded by dryons and black dragons. Inside it, is an urn that I must bring back."

"Why is this necessary?" his father asked.

"This is but the beginning of our fight against Cewrick and Zohmes. Obtaining the urn is the first quest."

"Tomas, I am going with Brenn," Laro told his son. "You are not to worry. Brenn will not let anything happen to me. I have asked Kira to come and stay with us here. I wanted to surprise you. She will be here tomorrow and will be with you while I am gone. That's with Brenn's approval of course?"

Brenn nodded. "Yes. My house is big enough."

"I am with you, too, Brenn," Ivran said, ignoring his mate's protests.

"I'll contact Aldis. I am sure he'll want to accompany us. We'll go on horseback. Erica, can you ride a horse?" He looked questioningly at her.

"Yes. I can. Oh, this sounds so exciting. I can't wait! But what is this forbidden forest?"

"The forbidden forest surrounds Cewrick's land and castle. The old legends tell us of a beautiful land, full of magick and wonder, not unlike the Clyss Valley. After the death of his parents, Cewrick hexed the forest and animals that lived within by placing a curse on the land. Anyone not protected by Cewrick will die upon entering the forest. We'll leave at sunup. I will instruct the kitchen staff to have traveling packs ready for us, wineskins and waterskins."

He quickly ate the last of his food, bid everyone a good night, and walked to his quarters, hoping that Ciara had changed her mind and to find her waiting for him.

No such luck. Sighing, he undressed and went to the bathroom bath. She had stuck to her word that he needed a good night's rest before heading out on the mission.

After he bathed, he contacted Aldis and told him of the quest and his new commission as commander of the first legion.

"Thank you, Brenn. The king wasn't pleased, but he understood. Of course I'll be by your side. I'll be at your house before sunup."

"Bring two of your most trusted and best. We don't know what we will find within the forest," Brenn warned.

He walked into his bedroom and to his surprise found Ciara on his bed. In no time, he joined her and, taking her into his arms, held her tightly, cherishing every small moment. "I am thankful you changed your mind and came to be with me tonight."

"I could not let you go on such a dangerous mission

without holding you, my lion."

"Your lion?"

"Yes, my lion." Ciara kissed his lips, nipped his chin, then gazed up at him with those luminous violet eyes. "Your lion will be your aid on this quest."

"You know I cannot—"

"Yes, you can. Rania burned the curse from you. You can change, and you will keep your humanity. Rest, my love. Sleep in my arms this night, for your journey ahead is one of hazard." Ciara nestled against him, resting her head on his shoulder.

He felt himself drift off, vaguely hearing a melodious song that almost sounded like tinkling bells.

CHAPTER THIRTEEN

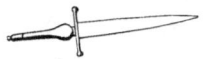

Brenn awoke before sunup. He quickly dressed, packed his backpack and his bedroll, and hurried down to the kitchens. It wasn't long before Ivran, Laro, and Erica joined him. They each packed the supplies the kitchen staff had readied for them, then dove into the fresh bread and slabs of smoked meat and eggs.

The suns barely peeked over the horizon when Aldis arrived, accompanied by Dunmore and Trevain. They all met in the courtyard and Brenn led them to the orchard, where Ciara and Icaras were waiting for them.

"Stand close together," Icaras said.

They huddled together and waited. Icaras began to chant while Ciara's eyes glowed. The dragon opened her mouth and breathed, but instead of fire, a stream of shimmering particles floated around them. Icaras' chanting slowed until he finally stopped, and the particles dissipated.

"You will be able to enter the forest now," Icaras told them.

Be safe, my lion. There are creatures in the forest that this spell will not protect you against.

Brenn ran his hand down the side of Ciara's long neck. *I will come back to you swiftly, my dragon siren.*

"I'd feel a hell of a lot safer if that magician could go with us," Erica mumbled.

"Magician?" Laro questioned.

Erica laughed. "Sorry. Another Earth word. We don't have sorcerers on Earth. We have magicians that do magic that isn't real."

"Then why do you call it magick?" Brenn queried.

"Two different words. Magic and magick. But no, we do not have anything like this on Earth. A magician is a pretend sorcerer."

"Then how can they perform magick?" Ivran questioned.

Erica sighed. "Ivran, it isn't real. It seems real to the people, but it is all trickery."

They entered Aldis' flyer and flew to the stables on the outskirts of Branton. The town was close enough to Cewrick's realm that they would reach the outskirts of the forbidden forest before nightfall.

"We will try to make the forest before nightfall so we should be able to set up camp within the forest itself," Aldis said as he readied the flyer to land.

"I agree. We can't cloak ourselves as we did the ships when we rescued our people from Cewrick. It would be better to be hidden in the forest than out in the open where his dragons and urcals can pick us off." Brenn grabbed his pack, bedroll, and supplies. "Let us hope renting horses goes quickly."

"I sent a message to one of my men in the area to have horses ready for us. I requested a packhorse as well. We don't know how far into the forest this cottage is," Aldis said as he grabbed his own pack and opened the outer door of the flyer. He walked out to retrieve the horses, followed closely by the two lieutenants, Ivran, Laro, and Erica.

Brenn stopped long enough to strap his sword to his back and followed them out to the team of horses that two of the stable hands were leading from the back stalls, saddled and ready to ride.

"Thank you, Orin and Balor," Aldis said, smiling at the two young men. "We can take them from here."

"Let's get the supplies loaded on the packhorse and get moving," Brenn said as he led the packhorse closer to the supplies.

After everything was packed onto the horse, Brenn selected a beautiful, dappled gray stallion. It wasn't Atom, but he would do. Brenn could have had his stallion transported to the stables. Normally he would have, but this quest was dangerous. Atom was a gift from his grandfather, and Brenn refused to expose him to the curse of the forest. Brenn mounted his horse. "Let's get moving. I don't want to set up camp after nightfall in a forest inhabited by Cewrick's creatures."

Brenn took the lead, the packhorse's reins in his hand, the others riding in pairs behind him. Because of the size of their group, he decided to skirt the towns and villages to avoid attracting unwanted attention.

Brenn rode in silence, enjoying the feel of riding again but dreading what may lie ahead of them in the forest. Nobody really knew what creatures were within its boundaries or what secrets could be hidden within. No one who had dared to enter lived to tell the tale, and those kidnapped along the edges of the forest were never seen again.

Soon, they came to an open veld, a huge expanse of tall grasses and colorful wild flowers, trees scarce. A pang of homesickness tore at him. The veld reminded him of the plains and fields near Xynnar. Far in the distance, he spotted the mountain ridge an ominous sentry standing guard over the dark shadow of the forbidden forest at its base.

They rode until the suns were high in the sky above them, stopping long enough for a quick lunch of dried harteox and hirthseed cakes.

Sitting beside the dirt path, Erica remarked, "Strange, we've seen no other travelers."

Brenn stopped eating and nodded. "Not so strange. No one travels these paths as they all lead to the forest. The black dragons and urcals have been known to capture those that venture too close to Cewrick's realm."

"Well, so far it's been quiet. Except I'm sure I see a black dragon high up above," she said.

They looked up. A small black dot circled high above them. "That could be the same dragon we saw when we fetched the blood from the clymm horses. It is almost as if it is protecting us," Brenn said.

"Or spying on us and reporting to Cewrick," Aldis grumbled.

"Cewrick's powers are waning now that his son is among us. Icaras will be ten times as powerful than Cewrick ever was. With each day that passes, Cewrick will grow weaker," Brenn reminded them.

"But that god will not," Erica muttered. "I keep seeing visions of a huge celestial being, ugly beyond words, with flaming hair, brandishing a burning sword and coming at us."

Laro looked at her curiously. "You have visions, Erica?"

"No, it's my imagination conjuring up this god and what could possibly happen."

"Then you had better stop that imagination. We'll face whatever comes when it actually happens. Sending the fear of Yanata into oneself doesn't help us on our quest," Laro told her.

"Yanata?" Erica asked.

"It is the name of the underworld where all evil entities reside," Ivran explained.

"Ah. Something like what we would call hell."

They finished their lunch and continued their trek to the forest. The closer they came, the sparser the brush and grasses appeared, until nearing the end of the day, they came to a vast empty space – the ground cracked and dry.

They stopped and gazed at the forbidden forest now looming before them. It looked dark, the trees black, bare of anything green or leaves, their branches reaching out like black tendrils of lightning. Reddish sap, so dark it almost appeared black, oozed from the trunks, spilling onto the ground and between gnarled roots.

"Are those trees even alive?" Erica wondered.

"They have existed for centuries, so yes. They must be. Cewrick destroyed what was once a beautiful land, corrupting everything that lives within this forest. Now we will test the protection spell placed upon us. I will enter first," Brenn said and rode ahead into the forest.

He held his breath as he rode a short distance before turning around and beckoning to his fellow travelers. He felt no ill effects, and no branches had reached out to yank him off his horse or slice him into two pieces.

"The spell works, as you can all see. What do you say, continue or camp here for the night?"

Aldis spurred his horse and approached Brenn. "We made excellent time. I vote we continue."

"I agree. Let's not tarry and go get that urn," Erica said and joined them, the others following her in obvious agreement.

As they rode deeper into the forest, strange sounds came from all sides and above, the crunching of twigs on the ground, branches swaying and groaning from a shift in the wind. Shrill wailing, sounding like women screaming, echoed to the group.

"This is really creeping me out. I expected a dark forest but nothing like this. I feel as if I'm in a Halloween horror movie," Erica muttered.

"I'll ask you later to explain that one," Laro said.

Brenn's horse stopped dead in its tracks, then reared, almost throwing him. He patted the horse's neck, speaking to the stallion soothingly, but the animal was restless and refused to continue.

Suddenly, a snake-like creature swung from the trees above, its mouth open, a forked tongue slithering in and out, slime dripping in a steady stream. Brenn reacted instantly. He drew his sword and cut the head off. With a *plop,* it fell to the ground, followed by a long body.

"Everyone, as you saw, eyes on everything, all sides, behind, beneath, even above you. Have your weapons ready at all times," Brenn ordered and spurred the horse on.

"What happened to the protection spell?" Erica asked.

"It merely allowed us to enter the forest. No human has ever ventured this far. Anyone that ever tried to enter was killed at the border between forest and land," Aldis told her.

It was but minutes later that Trevain was snatched off his horse. Erica fired her weapon at the snake-like creature, this one even bigger than the one Brenn had killed. Pulverized, its ashes rained to the forest floor, Trevain falling to the ground. Erica jumped off her horse and bent over the man. "Are you okay?"

"Yes. I did not see that tail coming," the officer sputtered.

"Mount your horses. I suggest we speed up," Brenn called out to them.

Urging the horses to a steady gallop, they rode on, deeper and deeper.

"How big is this forest? It didn't look that deep. It is almost like it's endless, or are we riding in circles?" Erica asked.

Brenn's horse stopped and reared again, whinnying loudly while stepping backward. Brenn looked around, up, but saw nothing. After settling the horse, he dismounted and carefully scouted around, swiping at broken branches with his sword. There had to be something in front of the horse. Cautiously, he swiped at the ground with his sword, threw a few branches, until suddenly the ground gave way to reveal a deep, dark pit. Brenn snapped his glimmer stick and held it inside the pit. At the bottom were large, sharp metal spikes. Anyone or anything falling into it would be killed instantly.

"Thank the gods for a horse that is so alert," he muttered. "One of Cewrick's traps. I am sure there will be more as we get closer to our destination. Stay close together. Do not stray."

Rather than mounting his horse, he now walked beside it, testing the ground with his sword. They had not gone very far when large, hammer-like boulders attached to chains began swinging from the trees, blocking their path.

"How does that arsehole even know the route we're taking?" Erica asked.

Laro shook his head. "Another unknown word. I think you mean Cewrick? He is a sorcerer. He's probably watching us as we travel."

"We will need to go around," Aldis said. "I also suggest we do not make camp within the forest."

"After we locate the urn, perhaps we can shelter in the small house the goddess spoke of. At least until daybreak," Laro suggested.

They skirted the section with the swinging rocks until it seemed clear, then returned to the original route. Brenn spurred his horse into a gallop. The forest was now inky black, as if there were no moons up above. Their glimmer sticks lit up the path they rode. Not too far ahead, Brenn spotted a faint glow. When Brenn looked at his timepiece, it was close to midnight. "I see something up ahead," he called out and slowed his horse to a walk. They approached and finally saw the shadow of a small house, its windows lit by a greenish glow that illuminated the trees around it.

They advanced cautiously. Without warning, two large beasts appeared in their path, growling, rising in attack, their claws extended.

"Dryons!" Brenn shouted. "Fall back!"

"Do not bother shooting at them. You'll only anger them," Aldis called out to Erica and the men. "Dryons cannot be defeated that way."

The two dryons stood before the cottage, now almost

hidden by the large beasts. A strange sensation coursed through Brenn's body. He dismounted.

"Brenn, get back on your horse," Aldis yelled. "We need to fall back."

Brenn ignored the words. Unstrapping his sword, taking off his clothes, he stood naked, instinctively knowing now what was about to happen. He could feel his muscles change, his bones pop, his skin stretching. As he looked down at his forearms and hands, he saw hair growing, his fingers turning into claws. For the first time in his life, his lion had surfaced. And it hurt like he had never felt. He felt his bones, changing shape. His muscles felt like they were being torn to shreds. The pain was excruciating until he stood on four legs when his lion had surfaced completely. Once the change was complete, it was strange—he could hear the humans exclaiming, could understand everything they said. He could think as if he were still human.

"Oh my god! Now I've seen everything," Erica yelled.

"Brenn, what have you done? You're trapped now," Ivran shouted.

"He is magnificent," Laro said. "A king of lions. Look at that mane! But I fear by changing he has lost his humanity. We have lost our Brenn."

He stalked the dryons, hardly believing the loud growl coming from his mouth. He felt so powerful, so mighty, ready to tackle anything. With Cewrick's magick waning, could he best the two beasts? Did he even want to fight them and risk killing them? These dryons had once been humans, lion shifters, possibly from his pride. He would hate to have to destroy them and wondered if there was any way to save them.

He had taken the dryons by surprise by his sudden change. They observed him first, then began to approach. Brenn slowly advanced, treading with caution. *You are not monstrous* beasts. *You were once human, lion shifters like me. I do not want to fight you. The sorcerer has cursed you. Can you hear me?*

It did not seem as if the dryons understood him, but they did not attack like the dryons he'd encountered before he entered the Clyss. They kept circling him, possibly sizing him up as their next meal. They were much bigger than Brenn, but he allowed his lion instinct to take over. After all, he had never been a lion in his life, let alone fought anything as one. He reared, growled, showing his fierce teeth. *My name is Brenn. We are here to find the instruments to defeat Cewrick and lift the curses he has placed. You are human. You were never meant to kill and destroy. Can you hear me?*

One of the dryons began the attack, but strangely, the other dryon lashed out and stopped it.

You have changed into your lion in Cewrick's realm. You will lose your humanity, and soon you will be one of us. Your lion body will begin its change.

So you can hear me. If I need to remain here as a dryon, then so be it. My team will continue the quest to defeat Cewrick and release all from his curses. Do not attack them. Do not kill them. If you valued your life as a human, then fall back.

Brenn stood on four legs again and waited. The dryons approached him, sniffed, then sat. The same dryon spoke in his mind.

You are sure the curse will be lifted? We will not harm you or your friends. If we could change to our human, we would help you in your quest. It will not be an easy task.

Thank you. My fellow travelers and I will rest here for the night. If I am to remain a lion and become a dryon, like you, I will remain here with you until Cewrick is defeated. But the goddess Rania placed a spell on me, so I hope I can shift back to my human. What are your names?

My name is Melion, and my friend's name is Shira. We once lived in a village called Xynnar.

Xynnar was my home as well. Cewrick destroyed it when he

kidnapped my pride. I do not recognize your names. You must have been here a long time.

Yes, we have, but I am not sure how long. I remember talk of Xynnar being destroyed. The one who ordered it was sent to these woods with no protection spell. It has only been a short time ago that some of my human consciousness surfaced. Shira is still evolving, but some of her humanity has returned, too. She was my mate.

I do not know how to tell my team that they can enter the cottage. I will enter it and maybe they will follow. Could you fall back and take up posts as watch? I am not sure what other creatures may be lurking in these woods.

Brenn turned around and faced the team. He walked slowly toward them, thinking about his human. The agonizing pain began again, his bones popping, his muscles changing and stretching, and before he realized, he was back as Brenn.

Hardly caring that he was naked, he jumped with joy. "The goddess Rania did it. I can call out my lion and change back to human!"

"You might want to put your clothes back on," Erica commented.

"I cannot believe this just happened," Ivran said, with Laro nodding and showing his disbelief.

"You two cannot change to your lion. Ciara told me the goddess blessed me and changed me. You will have to wait until the curses have been lifted, so do not even try it," Brenn warned them as he quickly put on his clothes.

He watched as the dryons each took up a post near the entrance to the cottage. Before he approached the door, he walked to each dryon and patted them on the head. "It will soon all be over. I look forward to meeting you," he told them.

CHAPTER FOURTEEN

Brenn opened the door. He looked behind and saw his team following hesitantly, glaring at the two dryons. The cottage consisted of just one octagon room. In its center stood an altar built from black rocks. Upon it stood a tall silver urn.

There it was, the object of their quest. Now, all they had to do was rest for the night and get out of the forest in one piece.

After placing their bedrolls, Laro was the first to break the silence. "Brenn, I cannot believe you were able to shift to your lion and back again. What was it like?"

"It hurt fiercely. My grandfather told me when I was young that the first few changes would hurt. But I was not prepared for it happening tonight."

"What did it feel like?" Ivran asked.

"Once I was in my lion, I felt so strong and powerful, as if I could defeat anything and anyone."

"You are a magnificent lion," Erica told him. "But now, more than ever, I still think I am living a hallucination. That none of this is really happening, and I'm reading a shapeshifter book. But if death is like this, I'll take it."

"You know, my love—" Laro began.

"For your information, I am *not* your love," Erica bit back.

"Sorry. Ivran and I are lions, too."

"See what I mean? Straight out of a shapeshifter romance

novel. The heroine falls in love with a shapeshifter lion," Erica snapped back.

"Ah, so you are falling in love with me?" Laro queried.

"Don't mess with my words! And you haven't proven yourself to be a lion shifter."

Brenn chuckled. "And he cannot. The curse is still upon him. Should he change into his lion, he will lose any semblance of humanity. At least for now."

"How did Rania remove your curse, and why can't it be removed from the others?" Erica asked.

Brenn clasped the pouch around his neck and smiled. "Ciara made it possible for Rania to remove it from me, and before you ask, no, she cannot do the same for others."

"No, of course not, because life is never that easy," Erica grumbled. "This whole situation can go to Yanata. Hah... I kind of like that. Yanata."

"She has the mouth of a space warrior, and the gods help us, she now has two languages to express it." Laro groaned.

"I knew there were lion shifters, but I never thought I'd ever see an actual change. You can't let others know of this yet. The bio-engineers might want to take pieces of you for testing," Aldis said.

"As if the king would allow it. But I agree, let us keep this to ourselves," Brenn said as a yawn escaped him. "We should get some rest. We have a long day of travel in the morning, and with our two friends watching over us, we can rest easy."

A loud crash startled Brenn from a fitful sleep. Looking around the cottage, he noticed the others had been roused as well. He quickly grabbed his sword and motioned to Aldis and Dunmore to follow him to the door.

Brenn quietly opened the door and walked outside. Now that he had changed to his lion once, he could see into the darkness much better than before. The dryons were still outside, but one was dragging what looked to be a body wrapped in cloth toward the cottage. The other dryon had the same type of cloth-wrapped item before it, carefully nudging it with its nose. A groan escaped the cloth when the dryon pawed at it to roll it over.

"What are you doing? What is in the cloth?" Aldis demanded as he headed out of the door.

Brenn stopped him. "Let me handle this before you make them angry. I would hate it if anyone got hurt."

Brenn heard Melion's voice in his mind.

Cewrick has sent food, though now that I have more awareness, I do not think I want to eat what he has sent. Neither does Shira. We think they are human. They have the same smell as your female companion. They must be from the same tribe.

"Aldis! Dunmore! Help me with them. Melion says he thinks they are human. Let's hope they are both still alive." Brenn ran to the bundle Melion had been dragging, while Aldis and Dunmore ran to the bundle Shira was nudging. Brenn cautiously unwrapped the bundle before him. Inside the bound cloth was a young woman of about twenty. Her lip was split and her face covered in bruises. He quickly checked her pulse. She was still alive even after the loud crash he had heard that must have been the bodies crashing through the trees.

"Laura!" he heard Erica cry over his shoulder. She was there in a second, kneeling beside the unconscious young woman.

Erica looked up at him, despair written all over her face. "This monster would actually feed live people to the animals? He's worse than the devil himself. Laura! Laura! Honey, wake up!"

Brenn watched as Erica tended to her crewmate. Laura was hurt. She could have fractures from the fall and suffer internal bleeding. How were they going to transport two critically injured people out of the forest? "Erica, she is unconscious. We need to pack up and head back to the city." He glanced over at the other victim. It was Mark. Why had Cewrick picked two of the Earth people to feed the dryons? Possibly because Erica was on their team to help defeat him? What had dropped the bodies? The black dragons or the urcals?

Mark had regained consciousness. "Erica? What's going on? Where am I?"

Erica left Laura's side to tend to Mark. "We'll tell you everything later. Right now, you need to stay very still. You were dropped from above along with Laura. Lord knows how many broken bones you have," she told him.

"I feel like I've been run over by a semi-trailer," Mark muttered, then groaned.

"Everyone, we need to pack up and leave. We have what we came for," Brenn shouted.

"How are we going to take these two with us?" Aldis asked.

"We will need to improvise," Brenn said.

We will help. We can each carry one of them.

Brenn looked up in surprise at Melion. "You will risk Cewrick's wrath."

Then so be it. We will help you leave the forest and carry the injured humans for you.

"When Cewrick is defeated, you will return to us. Do you want to risk getting killed?" Brenn asked, looking up at the huge dryon.

Under normal conditions, we would have moved on to the land of dreams many years ago. At least, if we go there now, let it be because we have done a good deed.

Brenn hurried back into the cottage, grabbed the urn, and wrapped it carefully in an oilskin. He packed it into one of the saddlebags on the packhorse. The others had already gathered their gear and were ready to leave. Melion and Shira picked up Laura and Mark with their large claws but were very careful, almost tender. Mark groaned. Laura was still unconscious. How he wished he had thought to bring a vial of Ciara's tears. Even with the help of the dryons, their travel through the forest would be extremely painful for Erica's two crewmates.

Mounting their horses, they set out to leave the cottage.

Follow close behind us. The forest changes each night, and we know the location of Cewrick's traps, Melion whispered to Brenn. Following the dryons, he trusted the creatures to lead them out of the twisted maze.

Looking around at the expanse of trees, Brenn could see the difference in the forest. The path they had traveled to the cottage had been swallowed up by a shift in the trees and shrubbery. It was almost as if the forest was a living, breathing entity. Gnarled branches reached down from above, almost as if they would pluck the riders from their saddles. Small streams of early morning light filtered through the branches, reflecting off the dark red sap oozing down the tree trunks, reminding Brenn of blood. He shivered in revulsion.

They made their way through the forest. No path remained to give their horses a reprieve from the twisted undergrowth and roots carpeting the ground. Brenn heard a whinny and the sound of a body hitting the ground. Laro's screams of pain hit his ears. Brenn halted his horse and jumped down to aid his friend.

"We need to get it off him! It's burning through his flesh!" Erica screamed.

Dark red sap covered Laro's arm, eating away at his skin and muscle like the acid dripping from a black dragon's maw. Aldis steadily poured a stream of water on it to try to wash the sap away.

Brenn heard Melion's voice. *You must remove the sap quickly, or it will eat away his flesh and bone.*

"The water isn't working," Erica cried.

"Here, try this." Ivran handed Aldis a wineskin.

Brenn grabbed Laro, holding his arm steady as Aldis poured the wine onto his arm. The sap slowly melted away, revealing severe burning in the muscles of Laro's arm and shoulder.

"We need to bandage this quickly," Brenn said as Ivran grabbed the medical kit from his horse.

Brenn held Laro steady as Erica and Aldis applied salve and bandaged Laro's arm and shoulder.

"Can you ride?" Brenn asked Laro after the task was complete.

"I don't need both arms to control the reins, but I think my horse's foot is broken." Laro grimaced. "His hoof caught in some of the underbrush and twisted, throwing me to the ground."

"His foot is not broken, but I wouldn't put a rider on him. The joint is weak, and the horse will not be able to withstand the extra weight," Trevain said as he led the horse back to Laro. "I have wrapped it to keep it from being damaged further."

"Laro can ride with me," Erica said as she wiped tears from her face with the hem of her shirt. "Let's get the fuck out of this hellhole before something else happens."

Brenn helped Laro mount Erica's horse behind her. "I am fine, love," Brenn heard Laro whisper as he headed back to his own horse.

Brenn mounted his horse and grabbed the reins. "Let's move on quickly. I am ready to be done with this forest."

They continued their way through the forest, the dryons effectively keeping predators away from the group. The fierce creatures had lived within the forest long enough to establish the food chain within its boundaries.

As they made their way to the edge of the forest, Brenn noticed the undergrowth and trees starting to thin and the appearance of four dark blue, almost black, flowers at the base of a tree trunk. Odd that they almost reminded him of the flowers that had sprouted when Ciara's tears had dripped on the soil. They were the same shape but much smaller, almost the size of a thumbnail. He stopped and dismounted.

"Why are you stopping to look at flowers, Brenn? We need to continue," Aldis said.

"I know. It's strange how these flowers suddenly appeared when all we've seen is dead undergrowth and trees."

"Never mind the flowers. We must make haste and get the injured the help they need."

Brenn mounted and spurred his horse, when Melion spoke to him.

Brenn, stop. The dragon says you must collect the flowers. They will help the humans.

The dryons stopped walking and gently laid their cargo on the ground. Brenn halted the group behind them.

"What dragon are you talking about?" Brenn asked as he looked skyward. Though there were breaks in the canopy of branches, it was hard to see anything that could be in the sky.

Hurry, you must collect the flowers. They are for the humans we carry. Cewrick tortured them before he had the urcals drop them. The dragon says they are dying. They are bleeding inside. They must eat the flowers, Melion insisted.

"Why are we stopping?" Aldis asked.

"The dryons are insisting that Laura and Mark need to eat these flowers." Brenn dismounted and collected the flowers. He grabbed a waterskin and walked to Mark, kneeling on the ground before him.

"Who is this dragon, Melion?" Brenn demanded. "I do not want to harm Erica's crewmates further by feeding them these flowers."

He does not remember his name, but he says you know him. He did not attack you when you left the Clymm Mountains.

Satisfied with the identity of the dragon, Brenn crushed two of the flowers in his fingers and placed them in Mark's mouth. "You must eat these flowers," he said as he held the waterskin to Mark's lips for him to drink. Mark grimaced as he swallowed the flower-and-water mixture, then turned onto his side and groaned in pain. "Why doesn't the dragon speak to me?" Brenn asked.

He cannot risk speaking to you, or he could jeopardize us all. The dragon and I can communicate without Cewrick hearing us. This became possible very recently. Hurry, the female is much worse. Feed her the flowers.

Brenn moved to Laura, crushing the last two flowers in his fingers. Gently, he lifted her head and fed her the flowers, pouring small amounts of water into her mouth to help her swallow them. Laura coughed and sputtered but managed to swallow what he had given her. "Will these heal them completely? Will they be able to ride?" Brenn asked.

No, the flowers will not heal them completely. The flowers are enough to keep the humans from passing into their dreams. We must continue. We are close to the forest edge. The dryons gently lifted the humans to continue their journey.

Brenn swung into the saddle of his horse and followed them. Gods, he missed Ciara. She would be able to tell him more about this dragon. Was he related to her? Could he be her cousin that had sacrificed himself for her safety? It had to be. He was the only other dragon that had escaped, only to be captured so close to the safety of the Clyss.

CHAPTER FIFTEEN

T hey rode straight through, eating while on their horses. To stop to rest was wasting time for the injured ones. They arrived at the stables after sundown. The trek back had gone smoothly under the protection of the dryons and black dragon. Brenn was surprised they had not encountered more traps. Cewrick had to know by now and be beyond furious that the urn was gone and his sentries had disappeared with it. Brenn also realized that the sorcerer's powers really had to be waning, because surely the man would have tried to stop them somehow.

We will leave you now. We need to find a hiding place where Cewrick cannot find us, Melion whispered in his mind. The flapping of wings sounded above them. Brenn did not have to look up to see. His instincts told him it was Ciara.

His beautiful lifemate landed close to him, bent her head, and nudged him. He planted a kiss on her nose. *I will take care of the dryons and the black dragon, my warrior. They will be safe. I will lead them to the Clyss. Before I leave with them, I will heal the two injured Earth people and Laro's arm.*

Brenn watched as she moved closer to the two humans lying on the ground, Erica hovering over them. Gently nudging Erica aside, Ciara bent her head close to Laura's mouth. A tear trickled down between Laura's half-opened lips — her breathing raspy and labored. Ciara did the same for

Mark.

Then she turned her attention to Laro. Erica quickly removed the bandages. Before Brenn's eyes, Laura and Mark returned to normal. Laro's arm healed instantly. Brenn had hardly noticed Ciara leave, or the dryons and the black dragon, he was so intently watching Laura, Mark, and Laro. When he turned to thank the dryons, Ciara, and the black dragon, they were gone. He looked up and saw Ciara high up, a black dragon following her. The dryons had disappeared completely. They had probably gone into the other direction leading to the Clyss. Now what were they supposed to do with the urn? What was its importance? And what would be their next quest?

"On Earth, that dragon of yours could make a fortune selling her tears," Erica mumbled.

Brenn looked at Erica. "It is a gift bestowed upon her by the goddess. It can never be used for gain. That is why these missions are highly classified. It cannot become known. And now, let's return home. We can all use a good meal and a night's rest. Tomorrow we will begin the second quest."

"Do you know what it is yet?" Aldis asked.

"No. Ciara will tell me tonight."

"You can let me know, Brenn. After I take you all to your house, I would like to spend the night with my family," Aldis said.

After returning their horses to the stable hands, they boarded Aldis' hovercraft. Brenn slipped into the co-pilot's chair and glanced out the front glass. Ciara and the black dragon were nowhere in sight. *Be careful, my dragon princess.*

Brenn turned to look at Aldis. "I don't think we should return Laura and Mark to their quarters. It would be better for them both if they were near Erica. I will house them at my estate for the time being."

Aldis punched in the location of Brenn's estate and set the

hovercraft to autopilot. "I agree. We will need to question them about their captivity. It will be much easier to do with Erica present. They may have seen something that will help us with Cewrick."

Brenn rubbed his hands down his face. The days and nights had been long and arduous since their ordeal began. "I will have their things sent to my estate. They were close to death when we found them. I will not ask them to speak about their captivity until they have been allowed to rest."

"Thank you, Brenn. Mark and Laura will answer your questions when they're ready. I'm quite sure they're shocked to the core at what happened to them, and it'll take a bit of time to get over it, but the members of my crew are strong individuals. We will do anything you need to help capture Cewrick and end this," Erica said.

Brenn turned to look at Erica. Laura was in her arms, her head resting on her captain's shoulder. Laura's body shook, and Brenn could hear the muffled sounds of her crying. Mark sat close beside them, rubbing the back of Laura's head. Brenn could see Erica really cared about her crewmates.

They flew the rest of the way to Brenn's estate in silence. Brenn rested his head on the back of his seat. He wished Ciara would contact him.

The hovercraft slowed, then stopped as it landed in front of his estate. He stood from his seat and grabbed his pack and supplies, then looked at Aldis. "I will contact you later and let you know what our next quest will be. Go home to your family and rest."

He followed the others out of the hovercraft's door, crossed the courtyard and walked into the front door of his home. Ciara had not made it back from the Clyss yet. He could not feel her presence on the grounds at all.

Worrying about Ciara and her task to lead the two dryons to the Clyss, he didn't tarry in the baths. What if Cewrick placed a spell on her and the dryons? Sure, the sorcerer's magick wasn't that strong anymore, but with Zohmes helping him, anything was possible.

Before he headed to the dining hall for the evening meal, Brenn checked on Laura and Mark. They each had their own room, and the bathing staff had washed them and helped them to bed. They slept soundly, obviously exhausted after what they'd been through. He asked the staff to keep an eye on them, but it wouldn't surprise him if they slept through the night without waking.

He was the last to sit at the dining table. "You didn't have to wait for me. Go ahead and eat."

"We've been waiting anxiously, son. Are you up to telling us about the quest?" his mother asked, sending him a glance filled with concern.

"I am exhausted. Thankfully, we all came back in one piece. I'm sure you've heard we brought back Laura and Mark, and Laro was injured, but thanks to Ciara they're all healed physically."

"How much longer before this is all over, Brenn?" his father wanted to know.

"Father, I have no idea. We have to fulfill a number of quests. Besting a god and a sorcerer isn't a task we can complete overnight. I'm just thankful we have Rania's help as well as Niqine's and Ciara's."

"Where is the dragon?" Tomas asked. "I looked for her in the orchard, but she's not there."

"Ciara is leading the black dragon and the two dryons that helped us to the Clyss, so they're out of Cewrick's clutches and beyond his magick. I hope she'll return safely soon."

"Dryons?" his father bellowed.

"Yes. They once belonged to our pride. Now, please, can I eat and then retire? Who knows what tomorrow will bring and I'm exhausted."

"And you know this how?" his father persisted, ignoring Brenn's words.

"They told me. One is called Melion and the other Shira."

"I know of them. They disappeared before you and I were born. They're our ancestors," his father told him.

"Now may I eat?"

CHAPTER SIXTEEN

The questions stopped after his request, and he was able to get some food into his stomach. After he finished eating, Brenn excused himself and before he left the dining hall promised he would tell them the full story and details the next day, then went to his rooms. To his surprise and delight, he found Ciara waiting for him in his bed. A new surge of energy filled him at the sight of her, and after taking off his clothes, he quickly joined her.

Holding her in his arms, he murmured against her face, "How did it go, my love? Are the dryons and the dragon safely tucked away in the Clyss?"

Ciara nuzzled his neck, stopping long enough to place a kiss on his jaw and whisper, "They are safely hidden from Cewrick."

Brenn kissed her softly. "Good," he whispered against her lips. He ran his hands down her back and cupped her ass, pulling her fully against him. "Because I ache to feel you in my arms."

He captured her mouth in a searing kiss. Then, sliding his hand down her thigh, he pulled her leg over his hip, his cock sliding between her thighs, brushing against her slick folds. He nipped her bottom lip and looked up at her. "I have missed you, my dragon princess."

Ciara held his gaze as her arms wound around his neck.

"And I you, my love."

Brenn turned to his back, pulling Ciara on top of him to straddle his thighs, then ran his hands slowly up her spine to her shoulders. The sight of her made him catch his breath. Her silvery skin gleamed in the moonlight from the bedroom windows. Her scales sparkled like gemstones, drawing his attention to her rose-tipped breasts. Slowly, he drew her down to capture a spiked nipple in his mouth. Sliding one hand down her shoulder to her other breast, he tantilized her nipples with his fingers and mouth until her moans of pleasure reached his ears.

Brenn stopped playing with her nipples long enough to gaze at the deep rose color his ministrations brought out, such a contrast to the silvery sheen of her skin. The sight of her made his cock ache to sink into her velvety sheath.

Brenn continued to tease her breasts with his hands, tweaking and pinching her nipples as he gazed up at her beautiful face. "Put your hands on the headboard and hold tight, princess."

Ciara grabbed the headboard above him and ground her core against his engorged cock. "Please, Brenn. I ache for you."

Brenn groaned at the feel of her slick wetness grinding against him. He captured her taut nipple one more time, then slid down until he could see the soft tuft of fur that covered her mound. Grasping her hips, he lifted her up slightly and tasted the sweet nectar of her arousal. Her body writhed against him as he tortured and teased her until her body shuddered in release.

Brenn nipped her inner thigh and slipped out from under her. Positioning himself behind her, he grabbed his cock with one hand and guided it to her tight opening, driving into her liquid heat with one quick thrust. The feel of her tightening around his cock made him growl in pleasure.

He leaned forward, placing kisses along her spine. Ciara moaned, arching her back to meet his lips. Taking her slowly at first, he reached around her torso to knead and fondle her breasts, then slid one hand down between her thighs to play with her little nub. Picking up the pace, he drove harder into her tight folds, with Ciara pushing back to meet his assault thrust for thrust, her cries of pleasure filling the air around them. Brenn bit her shoulder, thrusting harder as her slick heat spasmed around him, driving him over the edge with her.

Brenn kissed Ciara's neck, carefully pulling her with him as he rolled to lie on his side. Holding her in his arms, he nuzzled her neck and whispered, "I love you, my sweet sorceress."

They lay quietly in each other's arms, relishing just being together. Until Ciara spoke. "How did it feel to shift into your lion, Brenn?"

"It was painful, to say the least, but once I was my lion, I felt like I could conquer the world. I felt so strong, so powerful, I can hardly describe it."

"It gets better, love. The first few times it will hurt, but after you've shifted a number of times, it will come naturally. I would give anything to see you as your lion," Ciara murmured.

"I have a question. When I saw the book of knowledge, there was an image of a young peasant woman. She resembled Icaras. Maybe his mother? What does it mean? Is she going to be part of our quest to defeat Cewrick?"

"I don't know, Brenn. I will ask Rania. You now have the urn, and I brought back water from the Clyss. It has to be mixed with the ashes in the urn."

Brenn frowned. "That's it? I thought there were more quests."

"There are. The potion in the urn will not be complete.

Your quest tomorrow is to find an ogulim and extract one of its quills."

Brenn was shocked. Ogulims were large creatures covered in a thick hide of long white fur that housed bony quills filled with poison. They had huge claws that allowed them to climb the sheer cliffs and ice of the mountains they dwelled in. "You're not serious. Those animals live in the far reaches of the Cavaulal Mountain range, and you know how dangerous that area is. If the creatures are angered and shoot you with their quills, that's it," Brenn uttered.

"It can't be helped. We need the poison from one of the quills. It is one of the ingredients that needs to be added to the potion in the urn."

"What about the peasant girl? What role does she play in all this?" Brenn asked.

"I told you. I don't know. I will ask the goddess. But if you saw her in the book of knowledge, she must be of importance. What did she look like?"

"She's very beautiful. She has long black curly hair and gray eyes."

"I will speak to Rania this night and will tell you her answer tomorrow. Now sleep, my lion. Tomorrow's quest will take longer and be rife with danger. Where did you put the urn?"

"It's in my vault," Brenn murmured, feeling his eyelids grow heavy. *I wish she wouldn't place a sleeping spell on me,* he thought, but couldn't fight it.

Brenn woke up feeling completely rested. His bed was empty again. Turning to his back, he gazed up at the ceiling and sighed. *How long will it be before the day comes when I'll wake up with Ciara in my arms? When will our lives be normal and not fraught with danger?*

His thoughts drifted to the war he had just fought and

returned from. Never in his wildest dreams could he have imagined the path his future would take. Grasping Ciara's soul shard in his fist, he closed his eyes and whispered, "No matter what it takes, my love, we will win this battle and any others put before us."

He quickly left his bed and bathed, opting not to use bathing assistance anymore as it seemed to bother Ciara. After dressing, he hastened to the dining hall. Almost everyone was up and eating already, even Mark and Laura. They looked completely normal, as if their ordeal had never happened. It was hard to imagine these two had been on the edge of death less than a day before. Brenn noticed Aldis had already arrived and was seated beside Erica, discussing options for her crew for when they completed their transitional training.

"Morning, everyone," he greeted as he sat and began helping himself to a large portion of ircau eggs, smoked harteox slices, bread, and wraggia fruit jam.

Laro pushed a cup of dark, steaming liquid toward him. "Erica asked the cooks to make some of her coffee for us."

"Try it with the honeyed jago cream. It tastes even better," Ivran said, then took a sip of coffee from his cup.

Brenn poured some of the honeyed cream into his cup and stirred. Lifting the cup to his lips, he took a sip and smiled. Yes, they would have to start growing and harvesting this coffee soon.

He set his cup down on the table. "I have the details of our latest quest. It will not be an easy one. We need to retrieve a quill from an ogulim. Ciara says the poison is needed for the potion." Brenn heard the gasps from his friends and family. He knew the risk his friends would be taking if they helped him complete the quest. He watched Ivran's smile leave his face.

Placing his cup down on the table, Ivran glanced first at

Laro, then Brenn. "There is no antidote for ogulim poison, and in centuries, only two men have survived those mountains."

"How do you know this? If those mountains are that dangerous, why would anyone risk climbing them? How did you find out about the ogulims and what are they?" Erica asked.

"There were scientific expeditions many years ago to explore the territory. Those scientists never returned. Also, legend has it that centuries ago, before the ground shifted, when the mountains were covered with forests, a wealthy merchant lived among them, and he hid a treasure. The first groups of treasure hunters never returned, and the territory was deemed too dangerous to send rescue expeditions. The last group of treasure hunters that ignored all warnings set out not that long ago. Five men left. Only two returned and told the tale of the ogulim," Brenn explained.

"Now that you have all this-state-of-the-art technology, surely you're able to catch one of these creatures so that your scientists can examine it and make an antidote?" Erica wondered.

"The two survivors told us the ogulim is impossible to approach or kill. The creatures shoot the poisoned quills from their bodies faster than we can fire our weapons. Their coats are as white as the ice and snow and blend in with it. So the creatures are upon someone before one even realizes they're there. The three men that died paid for it with their lives.

"All we know now is that the poison of the ogulim acts as a nerve agent by disrupting the messages nerve pathways send to organs. Victims will experience convulsions and nausea and huge blisters from both inside and outside of the body, causing constricted breathing. When the blisters burst and fill the lungs with fluid, the victim dies of asphyxiation. The survivors brought back images of the creatures and the victims." Brenn knew they would have to take great care when extracting a quill from the beast. If the quill pierced the flesh and deposited a full load into its victim, death occurred within minutes, and from what the two survivors had told them, it was an agonizing death.

"And if you haven't been able to examine the beast, how do you know all this?"

"One of the survivors was a scientist. He saw the men die. After the ogulims retreated briefly, the two men managed to drag one of the bodies away. They brought it back, and our scientists were able to examine the quill and determine the cause of death, but they couldn't develop an antidote without the actual ogulim and the poison to experiment on."

"So this could be a double quest. We should try and capture one of them to bring back with us," Erica suggested.

"This will be far more dangerous than our quest to rescue Icaras. I understand if any of you have no wish to accompany me to retrieve the quill."

"You know we would never let you go on this quest alone. No matter how dangerous it is, we will accompany you," Laro said.

Aldis pulled a datapad out of his backpack and tapped the screen with the stylus. A close-up picture of the Cavaulal Mountains popped up on the screen. He pushed the datapad to Brenn. "This is our destination. The intensely cold temperatures alone could freeze a morcoug solid. We will not be able to land a hovercraft close enough to the cliffs, so you will have to climb the cliffs, rocks, and ice to the caves. The cliffs are too dangerous to hover above them and drop a crew down as we did when we obtained the sea serpent venom."

Brenn nodded. "I've seen images of the mountains. It's hard to imagine that many centuries ago, according to legend, they were once green with lush vegetation and flowers."

"What happened to turn them into an icy wasteland?" Erica asked.

"As I told you, there was a ground shift after which the mountains became much higher. The shift created huge, bottomless chasms within the mountain ridge, and after the shift, the mountains turned into eternal snow and ice."

"Ground shift. Do you mean an earthquake? You know, when the planet rumbles and the ground shifts? Buildings crumble into piles of rubble?" Erica asked.

"I suppose. It happened a lot in the past until our planet shifted orbit. We haven't experienced a ground shift since."

"What makes you think we will be able to approach an ogulim now?"

"Our technology has vastly improved since the last attempt at exploring those mountains. Talking about the dangers, I've made up my mind. I will not expose any of you to it. I'll go alone. I'll not listen to any argument," Brenn said determinedly.

"But you'd risk your own life. You'll not go by yourself, Brenn. We won't hear of it," Ivran said.

Icaras had quietly joined them at the table and now spoke. "No. Brenn will not go alone. I will go with him. The creature can't hurt me. I am the only weapon against it."

"Damn. Why didn't anyone think of that?" Erica said and grimaced.

"Icaras, we can't put you in danger. We need you to defeat Cewrick," Laro said.

Icaras laughed. "You are all forgetting something. I have come into my full magick. There is nothing that can harm me. Ciara and I have discussed this mission. She will help, too. There will be no more discussion. I am going, and I can protect whoever accompanies us."

"I understand your wish not to endanger anyone else, but we have to think about this logically. If you, Icaras, and Ciara can capture and contain the ogulim, I can have a hovercraft equipped with a holding cell and land it at this point." Aldis tapped the screen of the datapad and zoomed in to a flat cliff ledge halfway up a mountain.

"Can I come?" Erica asked.

Aldis nodded. "As long as you stay in the hovercraft with us."

Brenn took a deep breath and shook his head in exasperation. It was fruitless to argue with any of them. "Tell me your plan."

"I want to go, too," Mark interrupted.

"And me." Laura nodded assertively.

"No!" Most everyone yelled in unison.

"After what that motherfucker did to us, I want to get that son of a bitch and put him through a meat grinder!" Mark said.

"We understand, Mark. But you two need to heal from your ordeal, if not physically, at least emotionally. Take this time to relax, enjoy the surroundings, pretend it's a holiday," Erica said.

"Fighting that son of a bitch would help the healing," Mark was still arguing.

Brenn stepped in. "If there is any way you two can help, I will tell you. I promise. This mission will only involve Ciara, Icaras, and me. The others are merely going along for the ride on the hovercraft."

His words seemed to calm them, though Brenn noticed Mark still had an expression of disbelief on his face. "You deserve an explanation of everything that's been happening. My father will be more than willing to enlighten you today." He turned to Aldis. "Now, why don't we go out on the balcony to talk about today's quest."

CHAPTER SEVENTEEN

After finalizing their mission plan, they left the balcony to prepare to leave for the Cavaulal Mountains. Laro and Ivran reluctantly agreed to assist Aldis with preparing the containment cell instead of joining Brenn and Icaras to capture the ogulim.

Brenn quickly walked to his room and grabbed his backpack and sword and headed out to the courtyard below his room. Lieutenant Dunmore would be arriving shortly with their transport and supplies, and it would be his only chance to speak to Ciara alone before they left.

Brenn's heart raced as he caught sight of Ciara. Her beauty, even as a dragon, as always left him breathless, but he longed to hold her in his arms for more than those fleeting moments they were given in the late evenings and nights.

Ciara lowered her head and nuzzled the side of his neck. *I wish for it also, my love.*

Brenn traced his fingers along the scales of her neck, then stepped back to look up at her. "We only have a few moments. Can you fly in the cold temperatures of the mountains?"

Do not worry, my lion. I have enough of my magick returned that I can keep my wings from freezing.

Brenn heard the hum of a hovercraft approaching and looked up at the sky to confirm that their transport had arrived. The others had already gathered at the landing pad, waiting for Dunmore to land the craft. His attention turned back to Ciara as she nudged him with her nose.

Fly with me, my love. If we cannot hold each other as humans, at least we can spend these few hours together before we meet them on the ledge of the mountains.

Let me tell the others. Brenn took his communicator from his backpack. "Aldis? I'm flying with Ciara. Tell me when you're ready to leave."

"We're ready now."

"Good. So are we."

"Did you bring your skin suit?"

"Of course."

"Just making sure. I hope it's enough to protect you against more than a hundred below zero. Safe travels," Aldis said.

Ciara bent low so Brenn could climb up to her neck. He sat at its base and leaned his face against her soft scales.

Hold on, Brenn, she said as she exited the orchard. Within seconds they soared up.

Aldis just told me the temperatures in those mountains are a hundred degrees below zero or more. You can't go there, Ciara.

No. But I can land you near Icaras on the ledge. I already told you I can protect my wings. The temperature on the ledge is as much cold as I can withstand. Once Zohmes is defeated, the Cavaulal Mountains will return to their former beauty.

You mean to tell me that Zohmes caused the ground shifts?

Yes, he has always been an angry, cruel god. The human Zohmes killed was the rich merchant who lived on a beautiful estate in the Cavaulal Mountains. The legends of treasure are all true, but no one will ever find the estate because it is covered in ice and snow. Within its walls, Lord Tevrana Eertang built a stronghold that held his accumulation of wealth — gold coin, jewels, and other treasures. He still sits at his dining table, a frozen statue of once a great man, revered and liked by all. His servants, too, were frozen instantly. The cook still stands holding a platter of food.

How do you know this, Ciara? You speak as if you can see

145

through the ice.

Which I can.

How did this man anger Zohmes?

Ciara laughed softly. *It was because of love.*

Love?

Lord Trevana was to be wed to a beautiful woman. Her name was Sylveria Kefartu, the daughter of another wealthy merchant. Zohmes coveted Sylveria. She rejected him, and Zohmes blamed Trevana. He caused the ground shift and the lord and everyone on the estate froze instantly.

Ciara, you need to tell this story to our historians. It needs to be recorded. So what happens when we defeat Zohmes? You said the mountains will return to their former beauty. What about the frozen people?

They will awaken. But they will have much trouble adjusting to Ierilia of today.

This is beyond interesting. What a story to tell our children.

Ciara giggled. *Our children?*

I think we're here. Brenn watched the hovercraft land on the ledge. Ciara landed next to it. He slid down Ciara's leg. *I don't think the skin suits will be enough protection, Ciara.*

No. Icaras will also place a heat spell around you both. Be very careful, Brenn. Those beasts look soft and cuddly, but they are not.

Before the ground shift, were there other animals here?

Yes, many. Especially birds. They were of rainbow beauty.

What about predators?

None that I know of. This region, all owned by Lord Trevana, was a paradise.

So where did the ogulim come from?

They were Trevana's pets. Beautiful, white furry animals. Sweet natured and friendly. Zohmes turned them into what they are now to make sure no one who dared to climb the cliffs and somehow could survive the intense cold would ever find Trevana's estate and treasure.

"We need to put on our spacesuits and helmets, Icaras."

They entered the hovercraft and got into their gear.

"Be careful, you two," Aldis said as they left the hovercraft, quickly shutting the door behind them.

Brenn shivered. He could feel the heat from the skin suit, but it was no match against the intense cold, the freezing temperature penetrating through its warmth.

"Are you ready, my friend? Stand still for a moment so I can place a heat shield around us. The skin suits spacesuits aren't enough to keep us warm," Icaras said.

The cold that had managed to seep through the suits was instantly gone, and Brenn felt pleasantly warm. He looked up at the cliff they had to scale. It looked almost impossible. He began to remove the chisel from his belt so he could make holes in the ice, but Icaras reached out and, placing his hand over Brenn's, stopped him.

"We won't need those, Brenn. Stand close to me and hold my hand."

Brenn grasped Icaras' gloved hand and waited. He heard him chant softly. In less than a second, they stood on the other side of the cliff in a valley of ice and snow. He gazed at the peaceful scene and wondered where the lord's estate could be buried. "That was easy," he said.

"Now we wait for the creatures to appear. I am not sure if my magick will hold them."

Brenn grunted. "That's comforting to know."

"Ciara taught me the spell I need. But be ready with your weapon, just in case."

"Their quills fly faster than our weapons can fire. For now, I don't see any movement." Brenn scanned the expanse of ice and snow, but if the creatures blended that well with it, they would be difficult to spot.

Icaras nudged him suddenly. "Look. There." He pointed.

Brenn looked in the direction of Icaras' finger but saw nothing.

"They can't see us, but they can scent us," Icaras said.

"We're invisible?"

"Yes. When I took us here, I placed an invisibility spell on us."

Now Brenn could see what looked like a lot of moving snow, but as it came closer, he saw the creatures. On the images he'd seen of them, they hadn't looked that nice with all their quills showing. Right now, they looked soft and friendly. Their fur was so long it hid their eyes and faces. They resembled large woolly balls.

"Don't be deceived by their appearance, Brenn."

"Aren't they close enough?"

"Almost. There are so many, they need to be as close as possible for me to bespell them."

Icaras was right. Everywhere Brenn looked, the snow seemed to be moving. A knot started in the pit of his stomach. As long as their fur remained soft, they were safe, but that could change at any moment. He visualized hundreds of poison quills flying at them and shivered.

"Brenn! They smell fear! Don't worry. I am almost ready."

Brenn thought he saw the fur parting, but then Icaras held his hand up toward the creatures and began to chant. In seconds, the snow stopped moving.

"We can approach them now," Icaras said.

Warily, Brenn followed Icaras, who stopped beside the first ogulim. The points of the dangerous quills were still visible. "We've got one," he told Aldis.

"Good. The containment cell is ready."

"Come closer, Brenn. Touch the animal with one finger in a spot where there are no quills. I need to transport us back to the ledge," Icaras said.

Brenn noticed no quills on its ears, so he laid his finger on an ear. Icaras placed a finger on the other ear and chanted. In seconds, they were on the ledge.

"Step back while I put it in the cell. Don't want you in there with it." Icaras grinned.

Gliding his hands back and forth above the ogulim, Icaras transported the animal.

"That was easy enough."

"Now to wake the others," Icaras said and stood on the edge of the ledge. Brenn followed and watched as at least fifty or more ogulims woke up and sent their quills flying. Bewildered, they spun around, obviously wondering where their prey had disappeared to.

Ciara wasn't on the ledge. Maybe she had left because it was too cold, Brenn thought. They quickly entered the hovercraft.

After taking off his protective suit and helmet, Brenn looked at the tank. The ogulim was still asleep. It was really quite a beautiful animal. "How long will it sleep?"

"Until I remove the spell. The scientists need it asleep to remove a quill so we can add the poison to the urn."

"We have all the ingredients now. How are we going to administer it to Cewrick?" Erica asked.

"That will be my job," Icaras said.

"And then what? It will kill him?" Ivran asked.

"No, though he deserves to receive the death penalty for everything he has done. He is still my father, and I can't kill him. He will become the old man he already is and incapable of magick. He will be banished to Garissa Island. I have already discussed this with the king," Icaras told them.

"We also have Lord Quadra's trial by fire happening soon," Brenn said.

"Right. I had almost forgotten about him," Laro said.

"Quadra's crimes pale beside Cewrick's," Aldis commented.

"Why banish Cewrick to an island? That doesn't sound like much of a punishment," Erica said.

"Garissa is a small island owned by the gods. We are forbidden to set foot there since the beginning of time. Once Cewrick is banished to this place, he will be tied to the land and unable to leave, much like Ciara was tied to the Clyss. This will ensure he cannot escape. Even Zohmes cannot help him there," Icaras said.

Brenn looked at Icaras. "Ciara was able to break free from the Clyss. How do we know Cewrick will not be able to do the same?"

Icaras smiled in a way that sent chills down Brenn's spine. "Garissa Island is not the same as the Clyss Valley. Though the Clyss is blessed by the gods, it is still a part of our realm. Garissa Island is between the realms. It is of our world, but it is also a part of the realm of the gods. There will be no escape, and there will be no peace found for Cewrick. For him, the island will be nothing but horrors. No vessels can cross the parameter set by the gods."

"Then he will die? With no means to get food, he can't survive," Erica said.

"The gods will take care of all that," Icaras said.

"Has anyone ever seen the place? Maybe from above?" Erica asked.

Brenn nodded. "We have seen it from a distance from beyond the parameter. All we can see are dark cliffs rising from a turbulent ocean. They are very high and the summits shrouded in a permanent fog. Nothing else can be seen from above."

Erica shivered. "Sounds ominous. Has anyone else ever been banished to this island?"

Icaras shook his head. "We don't know. The punishment is reserved for those that have been gifted by the gods and disobeyed them and for fallen gods and goddesses. Stripped of all powers, they are helpless against the wrath of the gods and goddesses and doomed to spend eternity on the island."

"Yikes. Remind me not to piss off your deities." Erica poked Laro.

"I'm not even going to ask what that means," Laro grumbled.

CHAPTER EIGHTEEN

Brenn placed the cylinder that contained the ogulim's quill on the table in his dining hall. It had taken the scientists almost an hour to extract the quill from the ogulim's tough hide. Who knew something that flew so easily from the animal's body with lightning speed could be buried so deep within their skin. Luckily, the scientists had removed two quills without incident. One was for them to create an antidote to the poison. Brenn had warned them that the creature could possibly revert back to its original docile form later once Zohmes had been defeated, and the quills would disappear, so the antidote might not be needed. The scientists decided to experiment with the poison anyway and develop the antidote, just in case. For now, the creature was sleeping in the holding cell unharmed. It would be returned to its habitat later because after Icaras removed the sleeping spell, it would release its quills. It could not be kept in captivity.

By the time they had finally reached his estate, it was well past the evening meal. As usual, his cook had thought ahead and left a quick meal of bread, cheese, and smoked meats for them on the sideboard.

"How soon can we make the potion and go after Cewrick?" Laro asked as he grabbed a plate and filled it with food, then sat down beside Erica.

Erica grabbed a piece of the bread and cheese from the

plate and took a bite, then moaned in pleasure. "I'm starving."

Brenn, Laro, and Icaras helped themselves to food and joined Laro and Erica.

Brenn poured himself a glass of water and took a sip. "I will speak with Ciara after we finish eating. I think we could all do with food and a good night's sleep before we even attempt to discuss going after Cewrick. Besides, we will need Aldis and the space warriors on this mission. The rogue Toubosians are still in league with Cewrick."

"Didn't Aldis resign his commission as admiral?" Icaras said.

"Yes, he did, but he will not officially step down until the Toubosians have left the planet. There are still traitors in our midst, Cewrick's minions. The king has ordered that Aldis be in charge of the attack on the Toubosians."

"I'm going to retire for the night. Sleep well." Brenn left the kitchen and fetched the container that held the quill before heading for his quarters.

Her scent wafted toward him as soon as he opened the door. He set the container down carefully on top of the safe, then headed for the bedroom.

Ciara flew into his arms. "I'm so happy to see you," she said huskily against his lips.

"What's this?" Brenn asked as he held her at arm's length and gazed at her from head to toe. She was dressed in a gauzy, azure-blue gown. Gold sandals graced her small feet. The gown fell in graceful folds from beneath her breasts. It was adorned with tiny gold embroidered flowers along its edges. He was so used to finding her naked in his bed or in his baths that to see her in this finery had surprised him. But it was a pleasant surprise. Her hair was partially swept up, and she wore a beautiful gold necklace and gold bracelets on both wrists. A wide gold band with intriguing symbols was clasped around her upper left arm.

"It is time. With Cewrick's magic waning, I am now able to appear to your friends and family. They have not retired yet, so you can take me to the kitchen and introduce me. After that, Icaras will accompany us to your rooms, and we will create the potion and discuss a strategy."

"You are so breathtakingly beautiful. I am jealous of sharing you with anyone right now," Brenn murmured and tried to take her into his arms.

"Patience, lover. We must make haste, or everyone will have retired for the night."

"My family is not in the kitchen. I think they're already asleep. Only Laro, Erica, Ivran, and Icaras are there."

"The others are not yet asleep. I have summoned them to the kitchen," Ciara said.

"How?"

"By placing the wish to eat in their minds," she said, then smiled widely.

"That's not fair. They will all probably be in their night attire, and you arrive decked out like you're going to a royal ball."

Ciara laughed. "I am sorry. Would you like me to change into a nightgown?"

"No! You can see through your nightgowns."

"Then it will have to be my regular clothing."

"I'd like to see what your fancy clothing looks like if this is regular," Brenn muttered.

"They are all in the kitchen now. We should go," Ciara said while holding out her hand to him.

Brenn wished he could have recorded everyone's expressions as he and Ciara entered the kitchen.

"I thought you were going to bed?" Erica said, looking at Ciara curiously.

"I was. I would like to introduce Ciara to you all. She is able to appear to you now that Cewrick's magick is diminishing.

Mother, Father, Ciara is my lifemate and the woman I want to spend my life with."

"And she is a jewel dragon? I am so pleased to meet the woman who captured my son's heart," his mother said softly. She stood and, holding both arms out to Ciara, embraced her to welcome her into the family.

After the welcome and introductions, they sat and talked for a while and had a glass of wine, until Brenn said, "And now I really would like to retire to my quarters. Icaras, you need to accompany us. Ciara and you need to make the potion and bespell it, and then we will discuss strategy on how to get it to Cewrick. I will enlighten you all tomorrow. Sleep well."

"It feels so good to appear as a normal woman," Ciara said while sitting in one of the easy-chairs near the fireplace in his quarters.

"How long can you stay in human form?" Brenn asked.

"Until daylight. But as Cewrick's power wanes even more, soon I can remain human unless I wish to change into my dragon."

Icaras stood before the fire, gazing at the flames. He swiveled to face them. "Can we begin to make the potion now?"

Brenn opened his safe and took the urn out. He set it carefully on the coffee table, then fetched the container with the quill. "There you go. It's in your hands now. Be careful with that quill. The scientists have hardly had time to develop an antidote."

Ciara stood. She waved a hand over the container, and it opened magically. The quill floated out of it and hovered near the urn. Icaras removed the lid.

Brenn held his breath as the quill slowly lifted above the urn, then even slower tilted until its wider open end was above the opening. A substance flowed out that resembled melted butoro. Once the last drop was gone, with a movement of her hand, Ciara sent the quill into the fire with lightning speed. It happened so fast, Brenn barely saw it land in the flames.

Ciara reached into what appeared to be a deep pocket in her dress and produced a vial and a tiny knife. Icaras held out his hand above the urn, and she stabbed his finger. His blood dripped into the urn. Then she did the same with her own finger. As their blood mingled with the contents, white steam sizzled from the urn, spiraling up toward the ceiling.

Both Ciara and Icaras placed their hands around the base of the urn, spat into it, then began to chant. They were so in sync it was as if they had rehearsed the spell many times.

The sizzling steam rising from the urn slowly changed color, from red to green and finally to black. It spiraled back into the urn. Icaras grabbed the lid and screwed it onto the urn tightly.

"It is done," Ciara said as she sank into the chair.

"You both look exhausted."

"We are. To place the spell on this potion took a lot of our energy and power," Icaras said.

Brenn sat on the arm of Ciara's chair and placed his arm around her shoulders. "You both need to rest, but first, how do we get Cewrick to take the potion? He will not drink it willingly."

Icaras laughed sarcastically. "Of course not. Would you? Cewrick will know it is the end of his reign of terror and that punishment will follow. Tomorrow at first light, Brenn, you and I will transport to Cewrick's castle. Ciara will fly us there. She will hover above the castle until Cewrick is gone. After that, she can land and appear as her human. All spells Cewrick has placed will be lifted. The black dragons will once again be jewel dragons, and the dryons will be lions. It will be the same for all of those that were cursed. Everyone will be returned to their natural state."

"What about the urcals?" Brenn asked.

"They are Zohmes' evil creation. The surviving urcals will be banished to the island with Cewrick. After the banishment, the fleet can attack the Toubosians. When I leave here, Brenn, you need to contact Aldis, and he must be ready at first light. Sleep well."

Icaras left, and Brenn pulled Ciara to her feet. "Let me put the urn away. Can't be too careful," he said and quickly placed the urn in his safe and locked it. Then he turned and scooped her into his arms. He carried her to his bed and laid her down gently.

Before joining her, he called Aldis to give him instructions for the next morning. Climbing into bed beside her, he took her into his arms. "You are so tired, my love. Close your eyes and rest."

He need not have told her. Her eyes were already closed. Her head rested on his chest. He kissed the top of her head, doused the light, and tried to relax, but without Ciara's sleeping spell, his night was restless, his dreams plagued by images of an evil sorcerer turning them into pillars of fire.

CHAPTER NINETEEN

"**B**renn, wake up. Brenn!"
He struggled out of a deep sleep. Ciara stood next to his bed, her hand on his shoulder. "What's wrong?"

"It is almost daylight. We need to leave soon."

"Leave?"

"You are still half-asleep, Brenn. The urn, remember?"

That startled him wide awake. In one leap, he was on the floor, standing beside her. "Let me check with Aldis."

"I will see you in the orchard, Brenn." Ciara kissed him on the cheek and left the room.

Brenn sighed. Their time for being together and love would come fast now, he hoped. He quickly bathed and dressed, then grabbed his communicator and hailed Aldis. "We leave for Cewrick's castle shortly. Ivran, Laro, and Erica will be waiting for your transport."

Aldis' voice came through the communicator. "My men are ready to depart. The renegade Toubosians are to be killed on sight. Their empress communicated with the king. At first, she expressed the wish to capture the renegades and bring them back to Toubos to stand trial. But then she decided for her to attack them could be considered an act of war against Ierilia. Though King Biryn assured her he would not consider it an act of war and even offered her our assistance, she declined. Her reasoning was the renegades would receive the death penalty anyway, so she has requested their execution by us. The king was hesitant because this could be considered an act of war on our part. The empress sent a signed document bearing her seal absolving us and that we are destroying the renegades and their ships by her request and order."

"Good. They will be taken by surprise. Once Cewrick drinks the potion, there will be chaos as the curses are lifted. I will see you when this battle is over." Brenn closed his communicator, grabbed the urn from his safe, and placed it in his backpack. Then he left his room and headed toward the dining room.

Laro, Ivran, and Erica were already there waiting for him, their gear prepared and waiting by the exit, with looks of grim determination on their faces.

Brenn leaned against the wall after grabbing a slice of bread and cheese. "You can't go with Icaras and me, but I want you to go with Aldis to take down the Toubosians and retrieve the people from the castle that were captured by the black dragons and urcals."

Ivran looked up at Brenn with a determined grin. "Icaras told us this morning. After what they did to Xynnar and our people, I will gladly help Aldis rid our world of that threat."

"There is a kill-on-sight order. Their ruler wants them executed."

"There will be nothing left to send back to their planet," Laro said.

Brenn nodded in agreement and quickly finished his small breakfast. "Good luck, my friends. Aldis should be here shortly. Ciara, Icaras, and I leave in the next few minutes for the castle."

"Kick his arse, Brenn and Icaras," he heard Erica yell as he left the dining room. Brenn laughed to himself and shook his head. At least he understood what she meant that time.

Icaras was waiting for him on the verandah leading to the courtyard. Last night he had looked drained after bespelling the potion with Ciara, but this morning he looked completely refreshed, and Brenn could feel the aura of power crackling around the man.

Icaras turned to look at him as he walked out of the door. "Do you have the urn?"

Brenn continued walking toward the courtyard, Icaras falling into step beside him. "Of course I do. In my pack. I figured that was the safest place for it while we travel."

Ciara met them halfway to the orchard and lowered her head to nudge Brenn in greeting, then lifted her head to look at both Brenn and Icaras. *We cannot be sure how many of the black dragons may be slowly coming out of the curse. Be prepared for anything, including an aerial fight. The urcals will never turn against Cewrick. They'll defend him and his holdings to the death.* She kneeled and allowed them to climb onto her back. *Hold tight. I will need to use my magick for speed.*

"I will keep us seated on your back while you fly," Icaras said.

Brenn held on to Ciara as she crouched. She jumped, flapping her wings and soaring over the top of the orchard, shooting skyward, then leveled out in a fast glide toward Cewrick's realm.

Everything below passed by in a blur of speed as Ciara flew them to the castle. It seemed as if only moments had passed as she slowed and entered the skies above the forbidden forest. Smoke curled into the sky from dragon fire that set the gnarled trees of the forest ablaze. Black wings flashed, and fire spewed across the sky and at the ground as large urcal bodies crashed through the trees, the sound of their screeching cries echoing throughout. The black dragons, slowly regaining their memories, had begun their own war with the urcals.

Icaras, you will have to shield us from the dragon fire. I am going to have to fly through them. There is no way around it, Ciara said as she picked up speed to torpedo through the battle waging before them.

"I see some of the dragons regaining their jewel scales," Icaras said.

Brenn heard him mumble a spell, and they flew through the swarm of fighting dragons and urcals unscathed. From what Brenn could see, now that the dragons were returning to their natural state, they were much larger than the urcals, and the beasts could not fight against the dragons that annihilated them.

The ominous castle appeared below. *By now I am sure Cewrick is aware of the attack on the urcals,* Ciara said.

"Will he be expecting us?" Brenn asked.

He will expect something, but as Icaras approaches, Cewrick's powers wane more and more. Witness of this is the transformation of the black dragons and Cewrick's inability to control them.

They landed on the roof. Brenn and Icaras swiftly slid down and stood beside Ciara. A door of one of the turrets flew open, and six of Cewrick's minions rushed at them. Brenn reacted instantly. His weapon was in his hand in less than a second and firing upon them. Icaras held up his hand. A large ball of fire sent the remaining men tumbling to the roof floor, screams erupting from their hideous faces as they burned to their death.

Brenn carefully looked over the area to ensure no other minions approached them. Near the next turret, a battle waged between a dryon and the minions posted on watch. The dryon's armored skin and spiked mane was riddled with tufts of fur. More proof that Cewrick's power was weakening.

"Come," Icaras beckoned them. He led the way into the turret.

"Do you know where you're going?" Brenn asked.

"I remember the castle like I was here yesterday."

"Now to find Cewrick."

"I know where he is. He is in the vault behind the throne room," Icaras said.

Brenn heard a sound behind him and swiveled, weapon ready to fire.

"Brenn, stop, it's me."

She was there as her human, clothed in a lovely red gown and cloak. "Ciara? How —"

"Keep going. There is no time to waste. Icaras is very close to Cewrick now, and Cewrick's magick is almost gone. The curse upon me and my people is lifted."

Icaras stopped in front of a solid wall of rock. "The secret entrance to the throne room is here. My uncle showed it to me when I was young. I used to sneak into the throne room and hide and watched my father perform his hideous magick and spells."

"Why would you want to watch that?" Brenn asked.

"My uncle wanted me to so that I would learn how not to use my magick and that I should never become like Cewrick and use my magick for the wrong reasons."

"Didn't you tell us that your uncle trusted Cewrick?"

"He trusted him where we were concerned, but he did not approve of the way Cewrick used his magick and always warned me that when I came into my magick, it was only to be used for the right reasons. Uncle Geven never suspected that Cewrick hated me. And for some unknown reason, he had never told Cewrick that my magick would be more powerful than his until I began to come into them. But we are wasting time."

Brenn watched as Icaras bent and slid his hand into a crevice. An opening appeared at the bottom of the wall, just large enough for someone to crawl through.

"This opens up to the raised throne platform," Icaras said as he began to crawl through.

Brenn and Ciara followed and crouched beside Icaras behind the platform. They saw Cewrick pacing back and forth, surrounded by a throng of his minions. Once a man whose aura hummed with power and magick, Cewrick now resembled the old man he was meant to be. His waist-long gray hair hung limply around his shoulders and stooped back. When he turned to pace toward the platform, Brenn could see the once silver eyes that had sparked with dynamic command were now a faded, flat gray. Cewrick's wizened skin reminded him of old, weather-beaten leather. His clawed fingers clutched an ornate staff that he used more like a walking cane instead of the powerful object of magick it truly was. Cewrick stumbled on the hem of his black robes as he turned to pace the other direction. The sorcerer appeared to be as weak as an antaur.

Icaras and Ciara chanted softly in unison. Brenn could barely hear them.

But Cewrick knew instantly. He swiveled and stared directly at the platform. "Intruders!" he shouted.

His minions didn't move. They stood frozen in time. Cewrick swiveled again and raised his staff. He chanted, his voice gaining volume, becoming louder all the time as his spell didn't work.

Icaras and Ciara stood and slowly approached the old man. Gradually, the staff lowered, then pointed directly at them.

"Halt! I command you to stand where you are! Zohmes! I need your help! Zohmes!"

Nothing happened.

"You! This is all your doing!" Cewrick screeched and threw the staff at Ciara. In mid-air, it turned into a hissing creature, its tongue slithering in and out of its maw, slime dripping to the floor.

Ciara stood calmly while Brenn grasped for his weapon to kill the serpent. But it was unnecessary. Ciara raised her hand and the creature transformed back into a harmless staff that clattered to the floor at her feet. "I believe this now belongs to you," she said while handing it to Icaras, who laid it on the platform.

It was actually quite exquisite, Brenn noticed in a flash. Made of solid gold with many elaborate carvings, it had a large red jewel on top held by several gold claws.

Icaras stepped toward Cewrick, followed by Ciara. He held his hand out. Ciara placed her hand in his. Together they began to chant, and within seconds, Cewrick stood immobile.

"Brenn, the urn please," Icaras said.

Brenn quickly took the urn out of his backpack and rushed forward to give it to Icaras. As Icaras took the urn, Brenn noticed something odd. The amulet around Icaras' neck began to glow profusely, sending rays of light across the man's chest. A rumbling sounded. The throne room filled with light so blinding Brenn had to shield his eyes. When he slowly removed his hand, the goddess Rania stood behind Icaras and Ciara, a dainty hand on a shoulder of each.

Icaras lifted the urn, the lid magically turning and falling to the floor. He held it to Cewrick's lips, and the man's head tilted backward as Icaras poured the liquid into the man's mouth. After the last drop of the potion was gone, the urn disappeared along with its lid.

Within seconds, the castle shook on its foundations. Loud rumblings sounded. Through the windows, Brenn saw lightning and heard thunder, though the sky was an azure-blue. Ciara, Icaras, and Rania now clasped hands with Cewrick in the center. The lightning penetrated the walls and windows into the throne room. Brenn crouched to the floor, shielding his face. The thunder was deafening as the three surrounding Cewrick chanted.

When the thunder and lightning finally dissipated, Brenn dared remove his arm from his face and stood. The trio still stood quietly holding hands, but Cewrick was gone, as were his minions.

Hundreds of soul shards glowed brightly where Cewrick had been standing, belonging to the many dragons that had been forced to do Cewrick's bidding. Brenn gasped as a wave of blazing power filtered through his body and settled into an intense burning sensation at his chest. Closing his eyes against the blinding light of the crystals, he clasped Ciara's soul shard in his hand and knew without a doubt that the gods had protected her until the fateful night he had found her. If Cewrick had gained control of Ciara's soul shard, they might never have defeated him. When he opened his eyes, the soul shards were gone along with Ciara's. The small pouch in his hand was empty.

"It is done," Rania finally said, loosening her grasp on Ciara and Icaras' hands.

"Are all the curses lifted now?" Brenn dared to ask.

"Cewrick's curses are lifted. Your task is not over, warrior. There is still Zohmes to conquer. And Icaras, your quest, with Ciara's and Brenn's help, is to find the other half of your amulet."

She was gone as fast as she had appeared. Brenn was still dumbfounded by it all. "I didn't even have a chance to thank her."

Ciara smiled and moved to stand beside him. She took his hand and held it against her chest. "She knows."

Icaras walked to the platform and gazed at the throne while fingering the amulet resting on his chest. "What did she mean? How am I supposed to find the other half of this bauble? Looking at that throne, I am not ready for this. Brenn, do you mind if I live with you for a while?"

Brenn hesitated. "Icaras, there is much confusion in the

castle right now. Many of the people that Cewrick had under his influence were humans he had captured and bespelled to do his bidding. They will need guidance. Some will want to go home. Others may want to remain in the castle to work for you."

"I do not know how to deal with all that."

"Brenn, your parents and your people have no home thanks to the Tobousians. Your father is alpha, a leader. Do you think—"

"While the village is rebuilt? An excellent suggestion, my love, but it can't be a permanent solution. And I'm not sure my parents and the villagers would agree," Brenn said.

"You could suggest it."

"I can and I will. Icaras, you will need to address the people before you leave, but you are more than welcome to stay with me until you learn how to cope with your new role in life."

Icaras looked uncomfortable. "Can you help me?"

Ciara nodded. "You and I will go to the balcony. I am sure the people are gathered in the courtyard by now. Brenn, you need to contact Aldis."

"After Cewrick was gone, I already sent him the signal agreed upon via the transmitter."

Ciara grabbed Brenn's hands and stood on the tips of her toes to place a kiss upon his lips, then looked up into his eyes. "The dragons and dryons will be disoriented with the lifting of the curse. Many of them will not be able to shift back to human yet. My father will help the dragons, but the dryons will need you to assist them. Shift to your lion, my love. It is time to call the dryons to you."

CHAPTER TWENTY

B renn stood beside Ciara on the balcony, her hand resting in the fur of his mane as Icaras addressed the people, dragons, and dryons gathered in the courtyard below them. So many of them looked shell-shocked. Many would be haunted by memories of the atrocities they had been forced to do while under Cewrick's spell. Others would have to live knowing that their friends and family had died centuries before.

After shifting to his lion, Brenn had let out a roar of victory that called the dryons to the courtyard, though they could no longer be called dryons. In their places stood the magnificent lions they were meant to be.

Behind the lions and humans, a rainbow of scales glistened in the sun. So many different hues of color sparkled. The jewel dragons were now free.

Cheering erupted from the crowd as Icaras finished speaking. All around them changes were taking place. What was once a dark, sinister place entrenched by shadow and death was fast becoming lush, green, and full of life.

Ciara leaned down and rubbed her face against the thick fur of his mane, then whispered, "You are fierce, my lion, and surprisingly soft like an antaur. I could stroke your fur all day, but for now, I need the strength of my warrior's arms. We go to see my parents now."

Brenn licked her cheek, inwardly his human self grinning at the surprised expression on her face. He walked back into the castle and shifted to his human form. He quickly dressed, grabbed his gear, and joined Ciara and Icaras to meet the people gathered in the castle courtyard.

Brenn could feel the nervousness wafting off Icaras in waves as they made their way to the courtyard. With the support of Ciara, Icaras had handled the speech well, but after centuries trapped alone below, Brenn knew being among so many people made Icaras uneasy. "Icaras, you can return with Aldis and the others to my estate like you requested. The people that do not wish to stay within your realm are returning home, but there are others staying that can help until we speak with my parents."

"Thank you, Brenn. That is what I wish."

Ciara reached out and grasped his hand as they walked out of the massive castle doors. He heard her breath catch as she gazed out at the people gathered before them.

Brenn noticed a regal man with raven hair and violet eyes standing beside a beautiful woman with Ciara's refined features, but her hair was golden and her eyes the color of the suns. Both were dressed in royal finery. How they could transform from dragon to human and be fully clothed was beyond him.

"Mother, Father," Ciara cried and flew into their arms.

Brenn felt his eyes moisten as he watched the reunion between parents and daughter and listened to them.

"We always knew you would not fail us, child."

"But your memories—"

"We had occasional flashes. They were brief but enough to give us the courage to go on."

"Mother, Father, I want you to meet my lifemate," Ciara told them, disengaging herself from their embrace and returning to Brenn.

"Brenn, meet my parents. King Brokig and Queen Iede, rulers of the jewel dragons and the Tideless Abyss. Mother and Father, this is Brenn Mildash, general of King Biryn's army and a lion shifter."

"A dragon and a human? Unheard of! A lion?" Brokig exclaimed while Iede stroked his arm to calm him.

"Brokig, we saw flashes of this from above, remember?" Iede asked.

"I will not allow such a union!"

"Father, the goddess Rania has approved it. Brenn and I are destined to be together. Without him, you would not be free now. It is thanks to him accepting my soul shard that I was freed from the Clyss where Cewrick had bound me."

The king's eyes glistened as he listened to his daughter.

"Child, there has never been a union between a human and a jewel dragon, much less a lion. But if the goddess Rania has approved this, then I cannot argue. Brenn, I apologize for my rude words. Thank you for your part in our release and Cewrick's capture," Brokig said.

"Sire, I love your daughter with my heart and soul. We are bound forever. I would officially like to ask your permission to join with your daughter."

Brenn watched Ciara stretch out an imploring hand to her father and saw his face soften.

"If the goddess Rania has blessed this union, then so be it. From this day hence, you are betrothed. Ciara, you will return with us to our realm until the day of your betrothal."

Ciara squeezed Brenn's waist until he squirmed. "Hey, easy there."

"I will join you there tomorrow, Father, Mother," Ciara said and happily kissed Brenn on his arm.

"Tomorrow? But—"

A welcome interruption came from Brenn's communicator.

"Brenn? All Toubosians on our planet have been

eradicated. We have found the captured Ierilians and have them all on board."

"Aldis, good news. Cewrick is gone. All curses have been lifted, so almost everything should be back to normal. Except for Zohmes. But that's another matter to discuss. We will meet at my estate this evening for a betrothal feast. Bring your family."

Ciara looked up at Brenn. "Betrothal feast? Is your staff ready for this?"

"Oh, as soon as I communicate with them, they will be. Be sure to invite your parents and anyone else close to you. I can't tell you how happy I am right now!"

CHAPTER TWENTY-ONE

Brenn's staff had outdone themselves in such a short time. The great room housed a feast of roasted harteox and platters filled with fruits and vegetables. Beautifully decorated fountains of wine stood on each side of the banquet table, surrounded by traditional delicacies of stuffed wraggia leaves, cheeses, crusty bread, fruited tarts, and sweet-cakes. The room was decorated in golds, with two golden globes hanging from the ceiling in honor of Istus, the god of the suns.

The ballroom was decorated in silvers, to honor Asla, the goddess of the moons. Four globes hung from the ceiling, casting their silver light over the ballroom floor. Sprinkled among the globes were tiny sparks of light in the shape of stars. In the corner of the room was a platform with musicians playing all manner of music and traditional songs of the Ierilian people.

The rooms were packed with guests spilling out into the gardens and the balconies above. Brenn stood with Ciara and gazed over the crowded room. Erica's crew mingled with the members of his pride, many of them leading the Earth people in the traditional betrothal dances of Ierilia.

King Biryn stood off to the side with Niqine, King Brokig, and Queen Iede. Niqine would be leaving with the dragons for the Tideless Abyss to join Rania's handmaidens.

Suddenly a handsome young man with golden hair and eyes the color of a summer sky approached them. Brenn watched as Ciara flew into the young man's arms. A pang of jealousy hit him. *Who is this man?*

Ciara stepped back and turned to Brenn. "This is my cousin Taylith!"

Brenn heaved a sigh of relief. For a moment he'd thought he had competition from an admirer from her past. He held his hand out in greeting to Taylith. "Ciara told me what you did to make sure she escaped. If not for your sacrifice, Ierilia would be under Cewrick's power."

Taylith looked at Brenn. "And if not for you, we would still be cursed. I only wish I could have helped you more on your quests."

"You were the black dragon following us. It was you who left the flowers for Mark and Laura."

Taylith nodded in agreement. "Ciara, where are your parents? I long to see my aunt and uncle whole once again."

Ciara pointed to the ballroom. "There, with King Biryn."

"Thank you," Taylith said as he walked toward the stairs leading down to the ballroom.

Ciara smiled up at Brenn. "Come, my love. Let us escape before we are noticed."

Brenn quietly edged Ciara to the exit, then to the hallway leading to his quarters. "Now that is a mission I gladly accept."

Brenn and Ciara managed to escape unnoticed. He swept her into his arms as he kicked the door shut behind them. "Have I told you lately how much I love you?" he murmured against her ear.

"My father believes in the old ways," she murmured back.

"I understood. But for now, let's concentrate on us?" Scooping her into his arms, he carried her into his bedroom and deposited her on the bed. Wasting no time in taking off his clothes, he watched hungrily as she slipped out of her gown and lay before him naked.

In seconds, he was on the bed and gathering her into his arms. Their lips locked in a kiss filled with love and hunger, their desire so powerful in the aftermath of their victory that foreplay was far from their minds.

Ciara swung her legs around his waist and pushed up against his throbbing cock. He sucked her tongue into his mouth, tasted the sweet nectar of her breath, and tried to stall their joining, but she wouldn't have it. Reaching behind him, she cupped his buttocks and pushed his hips down hard until he slid into her.

Lifting up on both hands, Brenn tore his lips away and leaned over her, gazing down into her passion-filled eyes. Her parted lips were still swollen from their kiss. She had never before looked as beautiful as she did at that moment.

"Take me, my lion, take me hard," she said, matching his thrusts.

"I can't stop from coming." Brenn panted. "My love, I'm coming, I'm—"

Shudder upon shudder shook his body. Ciara squirmed beneath him as he came with a force that shook the bed and the walls of his house. She squealed as her release matched his.

Breathing heavy, his body still shuddering, Brenn suddenly realized the bed was actually shaking, and so were the walls. His heart thudded almost out of his chest as he pulled away from her and sat on the bed, gazing down at her. "Is this a special dragon treat?" he asked softly, but then saw her widened eyes and the look on her face.

"Zohmes."

Brenn leaped off the bed and ran to the balcony. In their passion, they hadn't heard the thunder or noticed the lightning that rent the sky. It was inky black outside, the moons hiding behind a bed of dark thunderclouds.

Another rumble. His house shook again. Several ornaments and vases fell to the marble-tiled floor, scattering shards of glass. Ciara had hastily dressed and none too soon. Loud banging sounded on the door.

Brenn quickly pulled on his pants and his tunic and hurried to open it. His father rushed in. "Son, you need to join your guests. They are panicking."

"We're coming." Brenn held his hand out to Ciara, and they rushed to the great room.

Erica ran to him as soon as they entered. "It's a fucking earthquake, Brenn. I can see your people aren't familiar with them. We need to go outside. What if your house collapses?"

"It's Zohmes. We have rid Ierilia of one threat, but now we have to deal with Zohmes' wrath at Cewrick's banishment." He ran to the far wall and sounded the gong. Instantly, the women stopped screaming, and everyone stood still.

"Please remain calm, everyone. Go outside and stay together," he shouted.

Ciara had disappeared, and he couldn't see Icaras either until the last people left the house. The two stood on the porch, hands clasped. He heard their chant above the noise of the shaking ground, thunder, and lightning. They were countering Zohmes' spell.

It took a few minutes before the ground settled, the clouds swept away by a fierce wind, and the lightning stopped.

Brenn hurried to join Ciara. Her face was pale, and dark shadows tainted the skin under her eyes. Icaras, too, looked drained. "You did it. You stopped the ground shift."

"It took a lot of energy, but yes, we overpowered Zohmes' spell. For now," Ciara said.

"I guess this ends our betrothal feast. It will be one remembered through the ages," Brenn muttered and watched his guests depart in their horse-drawn carriages and Aldis leaving in his hovercraft with the Earth crew.

Ciara's parents joined them. "Ciara, you are to come with us to our home."

"No, Father. I will stay here tonight. Brenn and I need to talk about Zohmes and what we are going to do."

"Then your mother and I insist that your betrothal be the shortest one in history for a princess and you be joined forthwith. Brenn, I hold you responsible for my daughter's safety. We shall take our leave now."

Ciara kissed her parents. Brenn shook their hands, then watched as they called out their dragons and soared away, their scales shimmering in the light of the moons. "I'm sorry, my love. This is not what we had envisioned."

"My parents will calm down. Let us go inside and talk."

Icaras followed them inside, and they headed to the kitchen, where Brenn's family had already gathered with Ivran, Laro, and Erica.

"Is it safe to go to bed tonight?" Erica asked.

"Yes. We have countered Zohmes' spell. He will be unable to do another for some time, at least not a ground shift spell," Icaras said.

"That was quite an ending to your engagement party," Erica said.

"Engagement?"

"Earth language for betrothal. Where do we go from here? When do we start fighting this son of a bitch? Though it's still beyond me how one can battle a god."

Brenn smiled at Erica. She would be a good fit as a warrior for the king. After the nuptials, maybe he should ask her to join his troops. "We have done all we can for tonight. All of us could use some rest after our quests and Cewrick's defeat. I will contact Aldis and the king after breakfast."

Ciara looked at the chaos in his rooms, a wistful expression on her face. "So many lovely things, all broken."

Brenn came up behind her and pulled her against him. "They can be replaced. What's more important, no one was hurt. Now come to bed, princess. Tomorrow, we plan for our future and the safety of our people."

The blade of betrayal cuts deep.

Sword
Of Betrayal

Crimson Realm
Chronicles 3

TARYN
JAMESON

GABRIELLA
BRADLEY

BOOK 3 IN THE CRIMSON REALM SERIES: SWORD OF BETRAYAL

When Erica is granted a commission in the king's army and a magical sword for her bravery, she begins to look forward to a future for both herself and her crew. But not everyone is happy with their circumstances.

Erica joins Brenn's team in the fight to save his planet from the angry god Zolmes, and she finds herself charmed by more than just the planet. The sexy lion shifter Laro, claims she is his lifemate, setting her passions ablaze. Stung by the sharp tongues and dissension of some of her crew, Erica pushes him away to focus on the lives of her crewmembers.

Can Erica accept a future with Laro, or will she let hate and betrayal decide her fate?

BOOK 4 IN THE CRIMSON REALM SERIES: SWORD OF JUDGEMENT – MARCH 2018

The blade of justice is a double-edged sword…

Betrayed by several members of her crew, Erica now finds herself in a race to beat the clock. A rare poison injected into the king's blood from the blade of her sword, threatens his life.

Erica joins her lifemate, Laro, and the rest of the team, on a mission rife with danger to search for the antidote to save the king. With an angry god bent on destroying the royal line by any means possible, the team doesn't know who to trust or what Zohmes will do next.

Can Erica find a way to prove the innocence of her crewmembers before the blade of judgement falls?

BOOK 5 IN THE CRIMSON REALM SERIES: TESTING THE CROWN – MAY 2018

A throne in peril. The crown challenged…

Born of love and hate, King Biryn must fight between the two. The demons within surface when the woman he loves is abducted by his great-grandfather, the fallen god, Zohmes.

Zohmes wants the throne. His abduction of Cylena ensures that Biryn cannot beget an heir. Imprisoning her in Yanata, the underground world of Ierilia and his to rule, he thinks he is one step further toward the throne and the surface.

Biryn must now face the biggest quest of his life, to defend his throne and crown. He has to travel to Yanata to rescue Cylena. With his team, his family, and the help of the god Izarus, he descends to the heinous bowels of Ierilia.

Will they be able to save his future queen? Can they defeat Zohmes once and for all and bind him forever to Yanata?

BOOK 6 IN THE CRIMSON REALM SERIES: SHARD IN THE MIRROR – JULY 2018

How does a dragon tell the woman he loves that it was he who had delivered her into the hands of the enemy?

Enslaved as one of Cewrick's feared black dragons, for centuries Taylith had been forced to do the evil sorcerer's bidding. Finally free of the shackles of slavery, Taylith is enlisted by King Biryn as a member of his elite team.

Plagued with visions of an impending war and the return of the black dragon he once was, Taylith must find a way to tell his lifemate, Laura, that he was the creature that had captured her and delivered her into the hands of the enemy.

To keep Laura safe and save her sister from Zohmes' clutches, he must allow the god to change him back into the feared creature he once was.

BOOK 7 IN THE CRIMSON REALM SERIES: INITIATION GENESIS – SEPTEMBER 2018

Starting anew on an alien planet, is no mean task — especially if that planet is rife with magic, shapeshifters, dragons, not to mention a fallen evil god, and a villainous sorcerer.

Now that the king and queen have granted the people from Earth their own realm, Bernie Henderson has been elected to rule it and oversee the building of their new city.

Zohmes and Odoxon have not given up. Bernie finds himself immersed in the trials and tribulations of Ierilia. How will this affect his budding interest in Julia, the mother of Zohmes' son?

Also available in September, **THE LION'S STOWAWAY**, a novella based on the Ierilian world and its characters will be published in an anthology with Viola Grace and other authors. Buy it at extasybooks.com and please help to support the authors by purchasing directly from the publisher!

ABOUT THE AUTHORS

Taryn Jameson is a mother, artist, and avid reader who lives in an enchanted forest that sparks her imagination to create. Her latest outlet is the written word. She is the alter ego of cover artist Angela Waters.

Gabriella Bradley is a mother, a grandmother, and runs a busy business. She has been a writer and artist all her life. Her hobbies include hiking, gardening, swimming, sewing, embroidery. Favorite movies are old timers like Gone with the Wind, Spartacus etc. Favorite TV series ire Fringe and Lost, Favorite music is Abba.

www.ingramcontent.com/pod-product-compliance
Lightning Source LLC
Chambersburg PA
CBHW071241130626
46556CB00003B/1108